# THE GOWK STORM

TO
*Tommy*
*"We twa bae run about the braes,*
*And pou'd the gowans fine . . ."*

Nancy Brysson Morrison (?1907–1986), was born in Glasgow and educated at the Park School in that city and at Harvington College in London. She came of a talented family who were known as 'the writing Morrisons'. Her brother Thomas and her sister Margaret both became well-known novelists like herself. A very private person who never married, Nancy Brysson Morrison lived mainly in Glasgow, but also in London and Edinburgh. Edwin Muir and Compton Mackenzie praised the 'poetic power' of her prose. Her work was also much admired in America, and indeed her late novel *Thea* (1962) was first published in New York. *The Gowk Storm* (1933), was a Book Society Choice, and was successfuly dramatised for radio.

An interest in biography resulted in books on a variety of historical and liteary figures: *Mary Queen of Scots* (1960) won a Literary Guild Award; *The Private Life of Henry VIII* (1964); *Haworth Harvest: The Lives of The Brontës* (1969); *King's Quiver: The Last Three Tudors* (1972); and *True Minds: The Marriage of Thomas and Jane Carlyle* (1974). She also wrote on religious subjects in *These are my Friends* (1946), a life of Christ in verse; *The Keeper of Time* (1953), a short book about the apostles; and *They need no Candle: The men who built the Scottish Kirk* (1957).

Her very readable novels, set partly in Glasgow and partly in the Highlands or on the fringe of the Highlands, include *Breakers* (1930); *When the Wind Blows* (1937); *The Winnowing Years* (1949), which won the first Frederick Niven Award; *The Hidden Fairing* (1951); and *The Following Wind* (1954).

*Nancy Brysson Morrison*

# THE GOWK STORM

*Introduced by Edwin Morgan*

GOWK-STORM. A storm of several days at the
end of April or the beginning of May; an evil
or abstract obstruction of short duration.

CANONGATE
CLASSICS
20

First published in 1933 in Great Britain by William
Collins Ltd. This edition first published as a Canon-
gate Classic in 1988 by Canongate Publishing Limited,
17 Jeffrey Street, Edinburgh EH1 1DR. Copyright ©
William Collins and Sons Ltd. Introduction © 1989
Edwin Morgan.

The publishers gratefully acknowledge general sub-
sidy from the Scottish Arts Council towards the
Canongate Classics series and a specific grant towards
the publication of this volume.

Set in 10pt Plantin by Hewer Text Composition
Services, 152 Leith Walk, Edinburgh. Printed and
bound in Great Britain by Cox and Wyman, Reading.

*British Library Cataloguing in Publication Data*
Morrison, Nancy Brysson
The gowk storm
I. Title
823'.912[F]

ISBN 0-86241-222-6

# Contents

# Introduction

Like Chekhov's famous play, and even more like the real-life Brontës whose story she told in another book, Nancy Brysson Morrison's *The Gowk Storm* is a tale of three sisters. These daughters of the minister, Mr Lockhart, are at the centre of the action, their closeness is emphasized, and when that bond is broken, first by the marriage of one of them and then by the death of another, considerable pathos results—a pathos which is never overdrawn or sentimental and which encompasses tragedy without making the whole book tragic in its implications. The family goes through the fierce and destructive April storm of the title, suffers sharp loss, but emerges with one moderately happy marriage and the prospect of a second.

The device of having the youngest sister, Lisbet, tell the story by reminiscence, works well. She is the quiet one, intensely observent, sensitive, sympathetic and imaginative, and slips readily into the role of what she virtually becomes—though this is not part of the story—a novelist. The only drawback of the method is that one or two characters with whom Lisbet is not frequently in contact—notably Stephen Wingate—remain less fleshed-out than they might have been; on the other hand, the women rather than the men are the core of the story, and this is no doubt the way Morrison wants it to be seen. Lisbet has another function too. Although there is a Glasgow connection (the Strathern family is Glasgow-based, and the action returns to Glasgow at the end), the story is set on the edge of the Highlands near the Ochil Hills, and Lisbet's vivid sense of her surroundings— the manse, the loch, the hills and trees, the birds and flowers, the weather and the seasons—creates an atmosphere that is both well-observed and yet deeply imaginative, brooding, suggestive, poetic. Her vision of the land is 'saturated with memories and legends':

> 'I thought of it submerged under the sea, of the ocean receding farther and farther from it; and glaciers creeping down the mountains, forming the glens and ravines; of the mountains as spent volcanoes covered by the impenetrable Caledonian forest.'

And she has visions of the future history as well as the past history of the earth. On a visit to St Andrews with her sisters just before Julia's marriage—almost the last time the three were to be together in any real sense—she imagines a desolate time to come:

> 'When I saw the sweep of sky joining the sea at the pale horizon, I thought of the light, waning to wax, imprisoned in the globe of the world. And as my thoughts ebbed and flowed to the drow of the sea, I thought of the earth after millions of years when life has left it, like a shell worn with holes, filled only with windy vibrations . . .'

The use of the rare Scots word *drow* (for which in fact the *Scottish National Dictionary* quotes this passage) to describe the melancholy distant sound of the sea, and the strange MacDiarmidesque image of the earth as an old shell riddled with holes, are among several instances where this domestic story of ordinary human emotions and relations is suddenly opened out into wider realms of space and time.

But the human story prevails. Julia the eldest sister, tall and dark, with a quick mobile temperament, falls in love with the new dominie, Mr MacDonald, who is knowledgeable and kindly and apparently calm and well-balanced. Yet MacDonald is credited with second sight, and he lives inwardly as a doomed man, a man (as Julia once said, critically) 'so sure of defeat he never went into battle'. Julia's foreboding proves true: in the freezing April of the gowk storm, taking shelter with the dominie in an old shepherd's hut, her head on his shoulder, she is horrified to see her father suddenly standing in the doorway, taking the whole situation in. She is even more horrified later when the dominie weakly says nothing and even begins to defend her father. MacDonald as Lisbet says, is 'afraid of happiness'. Julia's father forbids marriage, and MacDonald is dismissed from the school when it is discovered he is a Catholic. We can pity the schoolmaster; but when he slinks away at night, without trying to say goodbye to Julia, we feel that her father, narrow-minded and authoritarian as he might be, was not entirely wrong about the unsuitableness of the match. No comfort in this, of course, for Julia, whose mind in its sense of let-down and bitterness has 'gone like ice'. This, at the end of Book Two, is the first climax of the novel. The second climax, at the end of Book Five, involves the second sister, Emmy. Julia's crisis turned out to be a gowk-storm crisis, swift and bleak but not long-lasting; soon after it she marries Edwin Strathern, a widower with two grown-up sons and a grown-up daughter, and despite the difference of age and absence of passion, she settles down to an acceptable existence. Emmy's crisis, however, although it also takes place at a wet and stormy time, is not specifically identified with the gowk-storm, nor it is allowed any escape from disaster.

Emmy has a most attractive impulsiveness and direct-ness of character, yet she is the only one in the book's plot to have a human enemy (the jilted locum, Mr Boyd, who has his nasty revenge), so that her desperate love and eventual death produced that sharp but controlled pathos which is one of Morrison's characteristic notes. Emmy, unhappily in love with Wingate, her friend Christine's fiancé, is 'uncompromising', 'resolute and ardent', 'more alive than other people', and somehow vulnerable as her quick head movements toss the 'bright little curls on either side of her gay face'. The increasingly moody Wingate, irritated and bored by the clinging attentions of the pretty but vacuous Christine, whose indeterminate features are 'like a wax-doll's which have melted ever so slightly at the fire', breaks off his engagement. When Emmy who is in love with Wingate, and Julia who distrusts him, hear of this, there is a dialogue which shows Morrison at her most crisp and pungent:

'If you had become engaged to him and his feelings changed, you would rather he married you than told you?'

'Good heavens, no; but Christine would.'

'That's not the point. The point is that what Stephen Wingate has done is either right or wrong; the person to whom he was engaged makes no difference.'

'Don't look at me like that. I can't help it. I've had nothing to do with it.'

'But isn't it?'

'Isn't what?'

'Isn't it either right or wrong to break off your engagement when your feelings change?'

'I've not got an impersonal brain like you, Emmy.'

'It has nothing to do with impersonal brains. It has to do with right and wrong.' She began to tremble.

'I'm not Stephen Wingate's accuser, nor am I his defender. His own conscience will tell him whether he's done right or wrong.'

'You were accusing him just now.'

'I was accusing him no more than you were defending him. Emmy.'

'That's a lie.'

'Emmy, don't,' mamma cried.

'Say you don't like him now after this has happened, but don't say now you never liked him, for it isn't true and you are merely deceiving yourself.'

Julia stood gazing fixedly across the table at Emmy's face.

'I'll tell you one thing' she said slowly, after a long pause, 'that man and his emotions are not to be depended upon. He's shown that clearly. If he can do this kind of thing once, he can do it again.'

The hapless Christine drowns herself, and Julia's distrust of Wingate shows itself to be at least partially justified, though not wholly, when he devises a complex and desperate scheme to elope with Emmy, marry her by declaration before a witness, and sail off with her to rejoin his regiment in India. The elaborate logistics of the whole operation might just have worked, but for the sly machinations of the abominable Boyd. The painful realism of Emmy's fruitless search for some conveyance to take her to the rendezvous in time, and her fatal trudge on foot through wind and rain, are the most affecting part of the novel.

> Even after she was dead, her face quivered and the pulse in her neck leapt, as a feather sometimes gives semblance of life.

The Scottishness of the book is nicely managed through a combination of Scots-speaking characters (Nannie, Mrs Wands, the kirk elders) and a narrative voice which is in general English but which uses many Scots words quite naturally, somewhat in the tradition of John Galt (e.g. swee, fliped, Cloutie, craikie, creepie, howffs, gangrel, tirled, fank, sheiling, kelpie, wridy, scaurs, eardmeal). Scottish country superstitions are given an airing on several occasions, usually to be undercut by the robust common sense of Julia and Emily, but perhaps also to induce an intermittent suggestion of fateful forces working behind human affairs, as if the author had not quite made up her mind on this point. Even the last sentence of the book, simple though it is, has a thought-provoking ambiguity. As the carriage taking the Lockharts to Glasgow passes through the village, Lisbet looks back:

> The last glimpse I had of it was of the raised, hummocked graveyard on the hill, with its grey gravestones all blankly facing east.

The gravestones face to the east as an outward sign of the Christian hope of resurrection, but the fact that they stare 'blankly' seems to reduce the hope. The reader may also remember that Stephen Wingate, heart-broken in India, is himself in the east, leaving behind two buried women whose deaths he had unwittingly contributed to. Any suggestion of a reference to Wingate could only be a sub-text, but the fact that it can even cross one's mind shows that the generally forward-looking and hopeful conclusion of the story retains its suspension of the tragic.

Edwin Morgan

# Prologue

I can remember the trees in the garden at home. The manse was built in a very sheltered place, for to reach it from the road one had to walk through a wood, and it was shielded from the loch's storms by tall trees, stripped bare on one side by the wind. The garden was so full of trees they left little room for anything else. Yellow doronicums used to make a valiant show, and in autumn, amongst skeleton grey leaves, we found veined crocuses. Everything grew a little wildly in that muffled, breathless place. All the trees' strength went into their straggling height and each one seemed to be stretching upwards in an attempt to see over its neighbour's untidy head.

Most of the furniture was too large for the irregular rooms. It had come from mamma's home, and although some of it was good it had all seen better days, so that the manse was shabbily resplendent. The ponderous grandfather clock made the hall look uncomfortably small and on a quiet afternoon its ticking could be heard in every room of the house. Once, when grandmamma died, it stopped, and after it was mended by papa it always struck the hour at the twenty to. We grew so accustomed to it that other people's clocks seemed wrong.

Nannie also came from mamma's home where she had been nurse to her and her eight brothers and sisters in the days when the nineteenth century had been as youthful as they. She had shown a marked preference for the boys, to whom she used to give the white crusts of bread while she made the girls eat the black. But she was a Graham and let no man have his way. When any of the brothers had the mooligrubs or sullens, she would tell him she would whip him—ay, even if he were the Duke of Buccleuch.

She had comforted them in grief and watched over them in sickness, had rubbed butter on their bruises, seen that the adventuresome boys did not walk too soon, and sung to George and Frederick, long-since-dead Uncle Oscar and her favourite Octavius, when they were small enough to sit on her lap:

> *Here's a braw wee rascal*
> > *Straddling on ma knee,*
> *Clutching hand and kicking foot,*
> > *Shouting loud wi' glee.*
>
> *Are ye ready for the hunting-field?*
> > *And ready for the Race?*
> *Ready for dirk, dagg and shield?*
> > *For honour or disgrace?*
>
> *Ah, ma braw wee braggart,*
> > *Bide ye by me still—*
> *Time enow for your ain gait*
> > *And your ain headlong will!*

Papa, whose church was small and Highland congregation poor, could not afford a nurse, so that Nannie had to be maid, cook, nurse, rolled into one. She could not show favouritism between us for we were all girls, which I believe was a great disappointment to her. I could not tell which she loved the best. I think she was proudest of Julia, and she loved Emily because she needed the most care, and me because I was the youngest.

She was very wise and very strict; bread and butter, even on birthdays, always had to come first, and at tea-time we had to leave something over on the table for Lord Manners. Her voice was soft and had a Highland up-and-down intonation. When she wanted to say it was a stormy night, she used the word gurlie; when she meant some one was garrulous, she said wanwordy. When an apple was bad, it was wersh, and I was not the youngest but the shakings-of-the-pot.

We never grew older in her eyes. When Julia used to return, I think the sight of her was confused for Nannie by the memory of a little girl playing thoughtfully by herself at the fire; and when Emmy was quite grown up, Nannie always used to treat her as though she were a child too fond of her own will.

Her ay was ay, and her nay, nay. I used to weep sometimes when she would not give me what I wanted, and say that perhaps I would die soon and then mebbe she would be sorry. It was only the very good and the very old who died, Nannie, unmoved, would tell me.

# Book One

A pale green light poured down from the wintry sky, as though this earth were lit by chance rays from some other world. Grey sheep silently ate split turnips in the brown fields. The snow had melted in the low lands, leaving everything sad dun shades, and only streaked the mountains, where it lay like the skeletons of huge, prehistoric animals. The shouldering outline of the mountains cut against the horizon, their detail of burn, crag and ravine lost in the immensity of their shadowed bulk. It was as though, in those transient windless seconds between dawn and daylight, the world had resolved itself again into the contours and substances that composed it before man trod on its earth and drank in its air.

It was not yet breakfast-time when I entered the manse. I sat on the window-seat in the parlour and waited for it, looking out at the moss-covered garden wall and reading over to myself 'The Unquiet Grave' from my *Book of Songs*. The house I had left so still when I started out on my lonely walk was stirring now. I could hear Julia's raised voice in the room above and knew she was telling Emmy she really must rise, and Nannie's loudened footsteps as she swooped across the kitchen to snatch the boiling-over kettle from the swee.

Mamma was the first to join me in the parlour. She was a big woman and her step was heavy. Unlike papa, she was childlike in her faith; hope lit her exuberant heart and enthusiasms warmed her life, keeping her ever young. Her belief in prayer was unbounded and so had never failed her; now her confidence had grown to such an extent that she refused to contemplate even the most probable happening unless she so wished it.

7

She was still a handsome woman although she no longer paid any attention to her appearance. Looking back now, I realise, when I think of her carefree upbringing and lively youth, how uneventfully the days must have passed in the Barnfingal manse, yet she accepted them without question or regret, and never thought of herself as other than happy. But as she sewed at the parlour fire or sat at the table covering Nannie's jam pots (she sat to do most things nowadays), memories must have flickered in and out of her mind, like moths uneasily attracted to a candle-flame, until she would feel life was leaving her with nothing but anniversaries.

'I'm so glad the wind's died down,' she remarked, looking under the cosy to discover if Nannie had brought in the tea, 'I don't like to hear it—it's like some one keeping on arguing with you.'

Nannie entered with breakfast, stretching her long arms across the table. The effect the constant wind had on her was to make her always talk louder than was necessary. At the door she stood aside, in her crackling apron and wrapper faded with many washings, to let papa pass.

There was nothing rambling about papa's discourse as there was about mamma's. He said what he wanted as shortly as possible, then retired within himself to dwell on his own thoughts. His preoccupation was such that he only knew people by the places in which he usually found them. He spent most of the day alone in his study, with his papers, dictionaries and Cruden's *Concordance*, writing or collecting heads for his sermon on Sunday.

Julia joined us but Emmy was late, and I waited apprehensively as I heard her rush from place to place in the room above and pull out one noisy drawer after another. She came in when we were half-way through breakfast, and I saw her watch papa out of the corner of her eye, trying to estimate the effect her lateness was going to have on him.

'If this happens again,' he said, letting his glance light on her, 'you will go without breakfast.'

'I wouldn't mind going without breakfast if I could have a longer time in bed,' muttered Emmy, with a hidden defiance that I was terrified might flame into open insurrection at any moment.

'You mustn't go without breakfast,' said mamma, thundering into the breach with complications, 'you're just at the age when you need all the nourishment you can have.'

'You will not be late again,' papa declared coldly, 'therefore there will be no need for you to go without breakfast.'

At any other time his tone alone would have been quite sufficient to silence Emmy, but that morning she was ready to battle with any one, even with papa. She pulled at the collar of her dress, turned her face towards him and opened her mouth to speak.

'It is a beautiful text, papa,' Julia said smoothly, referring to the conversation Emmy's entrance had interrupted, 'one of the most beautiful—why, I feel I could write a sermon on it myself.'

Papa was always the first to leave the room after breakfast was over. That morning the door had barely shut behind him when Emmy demanded:

'Why can't I be late if I want to? It's my breakfast that grows cold and no one else's.'

'It keeps the dishes on the table and Nannie back,' said mamma.

'It's my hair that takes so long to do,' sighed Emmy, 'and it's not as though I had coils and coils to show for all the trouble it gives me, but there were tugs in it like spiders this morning, just when I was in a hurry. What was the text you were talking about, Julia?'

' "Be thou faithful unto death, and I will give thee a crown of life," ' Julia quoted in her softly deep voice.

'Yes,' said Emmy, after a pause, 'I like that. What do you suppose a crown of life is?'

'Immortality, of course,' said mamma, troubled in case an unorthodox meaning was going to be culled from it, 'it says life most distinctly.'

'It says a crown of life,' insisted Emmy, moving over to the piano, 'but who's to say that that means life? Anyway, what does the crown matter as long as you are faithful unto death?'

She began to play. Emmy was the only one who used the piano, and it was so inextricably bound up with her that I felt if any one else had touched its yellowed keys, no matter where her spirit lay, it would quiveringly awake and her fingers tremble to feel them once again.

In the afternoon papa, standing on a kitchen chair, hung up the print of 'Coming of Age in the Olden Time' which had fallen down from the stairway wall the previous week, making Nannie think the end of the world had come. We all stood grouped at the foot of the stairs, looking up at him, for when papa did anything about the house, he always liked people to be round him, ready with tools. He was straightening the picture to Julia's direction when a knock sounded on the door.

'Who's that?' papa asked us, quite unreasonably.

Nannie opened the door and found the ferryman, a mere paring of a man, without. He had been west at Dormay and seen two letters for us in the post office which he had brought with him that we might have them early. He handed one to Julia and one to Emmy, and would have remained, standing inquiringly on the step, as though anxious to hear their contents, if Nannie had not firmly closed the door.

'What pretty little envelopes—who can they be from?' Julia asked wonderingly, turning hers over.

'They're from Christine,' said Emmy, 'I know her t's—as though they were raising their hats. Oh, Julia, they're invitations to a ball. I never dreamed of such a thing. Won't that be wonderful? ". . . Desires the presence of Miss Emily Lockhart . . ." how lovely that sounds. Whatever shall we wear?'

Emily swayed dangerously as she stood on one foot and flipped her silk stockings. Her other foot was on the bed, each toe swaddled, like a mummy, in a different wrapping.

'You see, every pair of shoes hurts me in a different place,' she explained. 'Now, you are so much luckier than I, Julia, for your feet shape your shoes, but my shoes shape my feet.'

The bedroom was in exciting disarray with petticoats, dresses, shawls and stockings thrown over beds and chairs. A ball was an event that had come only once in our lives, and as I wanted to see them dressing I watched them from under the bedclothes to be out of the way.

Julia, being the eldest, had the use of the mirror first. She sat at the dressing-table putting the last touches to her hair, one side of her face lit by the candle's flame, the other in profound shadow. She was dressed in a maroon silk gown of mamma's that had been turned and which looked better now on Julia, mamma declared, than it had ever looked on her when it was new. Julia was clever with her fingers, but perhaps my inexperienced eyes endowed her gown with a richness and an elegance it did not in reality possess. I do believe, however, that she would have been noticed amongst any company whatever she wore. She was so tall, too tall perhaps for a woman, that she had to bend her head to avoid the sloping ceiling in the bedroom. Her carriage was superb and the wide space between her eyebrows and eyes gave her an expression of nobility, yet her face on any other woman might have been plain. It was her temperament that kindled hers into a spirited liveliness. It darkened and lit with her thoughts, she spoke with it as much as she spoke with her voice, until it was a joy to watch and killed every pretty face beside it.

A branch from the dripping fir tree outside suddenly whipped against the blackened pane, beading it with raindrops. Julia looked up.

'We must have that branch cut down,' she remarked, 'or one day it will break the window. Besides, it makes me think of ghosts.'

'Don't let's talk of ghosts,' said Emily, 'or I'll dream of them to-night. I wouldn't be afraid of a ghost of long ago, but I tell you what I would be frightened of and that is a ghost of the future.'

'Strange to think of us ever being thought of as living long ago,' mused Julia.

'Yes, that indeed will be strange; I'm glad I won't be living then,' Emmy said finally. She was running about the room in her stocking-soles, postponing as long as possible the moment when she would have to put her shrinking toes into her slippers. 'You know, if papa were wealthy, and I became engaged, I don't think I would like him to give me a ball. It's so like shouting your triumph to the world. Of course, I'm very glad Christine is giving hers. Do you think any one has been so excited as we? I felt almost ill when I thought something might happen to prevent my going. Do you know whom I think saw to it we were asked?'

'Nicholas or Martin?'

'No, that nice father.'

'Yes—perhaps it was. What do you think Christine will be wearing?'

'Something that will take all the shine out of me. And I know it was the father who thought of sending the carriage for us. It would never pass through Christine's head we hadn't a carriage. She would think you are born to have one as you are born to have arms and hair. I hope my hair won't blow about before I reach the road. Do you think I'm ever going to be ready in time? Where's my comb? I've lost my comb. Has any one seen my comb?'

'There it is, goosey,' said Julia, working her white gloves on to her fingers.

'Where?'

'Lying in front of you.'

Emmy put out both hands to find it.

'Emmy!' Julia said sharply, 'whatever is the matter with you? It's your eyes. Let me see your eyes. Why, you could swim in them. What have you been doing?'

'S-sh,' pleaded Emmy, 'don't tell any one, Julia, promise not to tell. I put in very little of the belladonna for papa's poultices—only a very little. I know it was wicked and I've been punished for it, for now I won't be able to tell one of my beaux from another.'

She could only see an indistinguishable image of herself in the mirror—as though she were looking at her reflection in rippled water, she confided to Julia, who scolded her all the time she helped her to finish dressing.

At last she was ready, with all her tapes and ribbons tied, her soft brown hair bunched into bright little curls on either side of her gay face.

'The man has come to say the carriage is here, Blessings,' mamma called up the stairs. She called each of us indiscriminately 'Blessing,' although, I am sure, none of us was praiseworthy enough to warrant it.

Nannie brought up my hot milk after they were gone and, while I drank it, she remained to tidy the room. Emmy's old brown dress looked shabby and lonely with its arms hanging limply over a chair, almost as though it had felt flouted by that glowing figure who had forgotten all about it as she ran from the room. Nannie gave it a shake and hung it up in the wardrobe. The excitement had upset her and she was uncommunicative, only answering my questions in monosyllables. So I looked at the milky castle peaks and milky brides at the bottom of the drained tumbler and at the skin, lined like a bat's wing, which clung to the side of the glass, until she was ready to go. She blew out the candle; the shadows quivered, then shrank and were obliterated by dark.

I lay listening to the scraping winds and piping creatures of the night. The fir tree touched the window again, only brushing it this time, making a sound like small tapping fingers. I fell asleep hoping Julia would forget to have the branch cut down.

I was awakened by their steps creaking on the loose board on the stairs. They had been away only several hours yet I seemed to have been sleeping for an eternity. I was too tired to sit up in bed to ask how they had fared and lay drifting on the tide between wakefulness and timeless sleep. One minute their whispering voices sounded jarringly loud, the next remote as in dream.

'Julia, you must have noticed. He paid more attention to you than to any one. He is so charming and distinguished—much better looking than either of his sons. Do you think he will be so very old?'

'He'll be forty and a bittock, as Nannie would say—yes, he must be nearing fifty. He said you were so pretty, Emmy, he wanted to pick you and wear you in his buttonhole!'

'He must be growing serious or he would never trouble to pay your sister compliments. Julia!'

'Yes?'

'What is the man like who is engaged to Christine? Every one's face was a blurred lamp to me.'

'He is good-looking in a young, fresh-coloured way—very fair and carries his head thrown back as though he were always breasting a hill.'

'He could not possibly know, could he, that I had done something to my eyes?'

'It's most unlikely. Why?'

'I felt he was staring so, even when I was not looking, but perhaps it was only my imagination. Anyway it doesn't matter.'

There was silence for a space and I was about to slip into oblivion when Julia's shocked voice recalled me.

'Emmy! you can't leave your clothes like that.'

'Oh, yes, I can and I am going to,' I heard my younger sister rejoin, and the sheets tugged as she climbed in beside me.

Papa and mamma were paying their annual visit to Dr Malcolm on the other side of the loch, and the three of us sat with Nannie in the kitchen, as we had done since we had been children on the rare occasions they left the manse.

The leaping flames in the well of a fireplace lit the room, casting grotesque shadows on the raftered roof and walls, exaggerating Nannie's hooked nose and the peaks of her cap. Her brow was so deeply furrowed it looked cut, but the rest of her face was unlined. As she sat at the fireside, a ball of wool stuck with knitting-pins on her lap, she looked as though at any moment she might go up the chimney in a whiff of smoke, leaving behind only two wrinkled boots with their laces out.

'Do you think,' said Emmy, 'that the clock bothers striking when every one is asleep?' She had toothache and was nursing her cheek on her arm. 'Where do you think pain goes when it leaves you? I wish I was made of nothing and then I would have nothing to ache. I wish—I wish—oh, so many things!'

'There's no guid wishing your whole life awa',' remarked Nannie. 'Time flies quicker than the deil kens.'

'What is the very first thing you can remember, Nannie?' Julia asked pensively.

'The cockleshell on the window-sill and ma brither eating a bannock and no giving me any o' it.'

'The first thing *I* can remember,' said Julia, 'is papa rehearsing with zest his sermon before mamma.'

'Ay, I mind that,' Nannie said reminiscently, 'and ye keppit up wi' his voice wi' your spoon on the table until he had to check ye.'

'The first thing I remember,' put in Emmy, 'was wakening up mamma when she dozed to go on singing me to sleep.'

'One of the first things I can remember,' I said, 'was the strip of light, like an upside-down L, on our bedroom wall at night which widened when the door was opened farther.'

I did not care to tell them, for some unknown reason, of my earliest memories when I used to lie in bed in the early morning and trace forms in the scrolled pitch pine of the mantelpiece. Then I would lie so motionless I might have been asleep or dead while I said over and over to myself, 'What am I? Who am I? What am I?' And always on the brink of discovery, when I had reached that peak where deadly knowledge lay just within grasp, I would bring myself, in the nick of time, with a breathless jerk back to bed.

'Isn't it sad to think,' Julia said after a pause, 'that every one, no matter how bad, can remember a time, at the beginning of things, when he didn't know what evil was?'

'I'm too auld in the horn to waste muckle sorrow on the bad,' Nannie told her in her emphatic manner; 'every man on this earth has his chance and it's his ain loss if he willna tak' it. But he may have ta'en it for a' we are to ken. It's no if ye win through that counts, it's the warsle that it costs ye.'

'But people change so, don't they, Nannie?' asked Julia.

'If ye can change for the bad, ye can change for the guid.'

'I wasn't thinking of change in that way,' said Julia. 'But take papa, for instance—why, I can remember when he was as gay as a fiddle the whole day long. Life seems to turn you out quite differently from what you or any one else expect.'

'That's because ye get too used to it, and tak' it as your due. Ye should bide as though to-day was mebbe going to be your last, and then ye wouldna be tethered to this earth wi' things that graw bigger to ye than life itsel'.'

The log in the fireplace subsided and a shower of sparks shot up the soot-furred chimney.

'I can see soldiers in the fire,' Julia said dreamily, her eyes half-closed, 'a whole column of them, and they fired their muskets just now.'

'Christine's future husband is a soldier,' observed Emmy, sitting on the table and leaning her cheek against the window-pane. 'Would you like to be married to a soldier? I think I would, and share, even afar off, his danger. You know, it must have been stirring to have lived long ago and seen them go out to battle to the wild crying of the pipes.'

'It's only auld maids wha sit on tables,' remarked Nannie.

'The heat makes my tooth sorer,' moaned Emmy, sliding from the table, 'and cold seems to help it.'

'Poor Emmy!' Julia said pityingly.

'I wonder if I would mind being an old maid,' reflected Emmy. 'You remember poor old Tibby MacNaughton whispering to mamma, who thought she was Mrs Mac-Naughton, "I'm only Miss, but I'm getting o'er it noo a wee."'

'There's worse things than being an auld maid,' said Nannie, heating a shawl at the fire to wrap round Emmy's cheek. 'Marriage ne'er yet cured ill temper and self-mindedness. Ma graundmither used to say lang-back-seen, "Ne'er marry for siller or ye'll carry a heart heavy as gold and always mind that 'mithers' laddies' mak' the puirest husbands."'

'Christine once burst into tears because she had four gean-stones on her plate,' said Emmy; 'it would take more than that to make me cry.' She joined us again in the glow of firelight which linked us all together and Nannie bound her face in the shawl.

The kettle on the swee began to sing. I sat on the creepie, drowsy and content. Outside early dark had folded away the garden and the winds were beating through the glen like the coming of the Campbells. But within there was flickering flame and singing kettle, and light shining on the window-pane to signal brightly between the trees to some sacred stranger without.

Visitors who came to the manse were discussed later in detail by the three of us as we sat round the fire in the evening. We saw so few people that we were inclined to magnify the faults or virtues of those who did come, either enjoying their company out of all proportion or exaggerating their foibles. There was little that evaded Emily's astute analysis or escaped Julia's glance, while I listened to the ecclesiastical views of Mr Urquhart, papa's clerical friend, with an absorption I now realise was quite unwarranted.

One afternoon, some weeks after the ball, two visitors, neither of whom I had seen before, paid us a surprise call. They were Christine Strathern and her father who had come to ask my sisters to drink tea with them that afternoon. Mamma was in bed with a bad chill and papa was officiating at a funeral, so while Julia and Emmy put on their outdoor clothes, I sat alone with our guests in the parlour. I could find nothing to say to them but, while the clock's ticking claimed the silence, I saw everything there was to note about the father and daughter.

Most kind he looked with a benignant brow. I knew his thoughts were elsewhere for he did not seem to know that I sat there, but sometimes frowned and looked about him and at others seemed to listen. She was little and fair, her small face poking forward under her bonnet. Her features were so indeterminate they made no impression upon me; they were like a wax-doll's which have melted ever so slightly at the fire. Yet she made a charming enough picture in her brown coat with its little capes edged with fur. For the first time I was conscious that Julia's dress was too big for me and my shoe buttons did not match. I felt myself, for some unaccountable reason, begin to blush.

He suddenly sat back in his chair until it creaked and smiled as though seeing me for the first time. Then he rose and stood looking out of the window.

'You must be very near the loch,' he remarked. 'It never floods your garden, does it?'

I stood beside him in my eagerness to answer.

'Once it did,' I said, 'when I was very small—a long, long time ago.'

I saw him smile, I knew not why.

'And you,' he asked, as though struck by some unspoken thought, 'have you been away to school or have you always lived here?'

'Papa taught Julia,' I replied, 'and Julia taught Emmy and me.'

'You are very like—Julia,' he said, looking down at me closely.

'Julia and I are supposed to be like papa,' I informed him, 'and Emmy like what mamma used to be.'

He bowed in acquiescence. At that moment Julia entered and all was ease again. Christine rose and fluttered to her like a little chaffinch.

'How hidden you are down here, Juley—we all but missed the gate.'

'We had to come through the wood to find you, Miss Julia,' he said, and the look he bent on her made my heart leap.

When Emily came down the stairs, they prepared to depart. I was harassed, not knowing whether I should shake hands with Christine or her father first; then, because I liked him so much the better, I advanced towards him.

'But what is this?' he asked. 'You are surely coming with us, certainly you are. You know, I never knew until this afternoon there was another sister. There are no more of you hiding away, are there? And if they ever leave you at home again, I'll come to fetch you myself.'

We all walked up the path together through the wood to the gate where the grasses that grew at the foot of the dyke and the mosses that clung to its rough stones were the vivid, intense green of things that grow in shaded places. The manse burn, deep as a river, fell far below in its gorge bed with a sound like eternal thunder. The sun struck wildly between the trees, and the shadows of their boles striped the ground.

It was a pleasurable sensation to sit in the carriage and pass all the places which we passed in our everyday walks and which now seemed so unfamiliar. Well-known landmarks looked inconspicuous and we came upon them so swiftly that I felt the road that afternoon was like a shrunken measuring-tape.

The kindly sun glanced on the sullen hill-tops and lit up every blade of grass growing from the tussocky dykes. In its light a sprouting ash looked unearthly beside a ploughed field and the silver birches, with their leafless fronds, were like petrified falling rain. At the sound of the wheels the bleating lambs ran unsteadily to their mothers. Emmy and I always thought lambs had such wise little faces to grow into silly sheep.

It was a drive of some eight miles to the Stratherns' house, which stood on a hill overlooking the valley of the Dorm. The river, blue as the cold spring sky above, wound through the desolate glen between low red banks, which made me picture Jeremiah digging up his girdle on the shore of the Euphrates, of the kings who came to war against Joshua pitching by the waters of Merom, and of god-lit Elijah standing by Jordan.

The gates were open and the carriage passed slowly between two green-stained pillars each of which was topped by a round stone marked to represent a crude face, two circles doing duty for eyes and a curved stroke forming the mouth. The avenue approached the dwelling from the side so that much of the house's effect was lost. It is a curious thing that, although in the days to come I often visited and even lived there for some weeks, I have no picture in my mind of the house as a whole. I can remember parts of it as vividly as though I had seen it only yesterday, yet I have no recollection whatsoever of its outline.

It had been built less than a century ago. Mr Strathern was the heir of a long line of merchants who had imported tobacco from America, the trade that made Glasgow. He often wearied of his home in Virginia Place and so some years ago had bought Gel Lodge where he and his family could spend their long and frequent holidays.

If I had no impression of the house from without, I, who was easily awed, had a distinct impression of richness and grandeur whenever I entered. We were taken into the drawing-room where the view was hidden from us by heavy curtains. Mr Strathern was a widower and I was introduced to his sister who had looked after his household since his wife's death many years ago. Two other people stood there: Nicholas, the elder son, a handsome, angry-looking man with slightly distended nostrils like those of a rocking-horse, and Martin, who was too stout for his twenty-three years and who looked as though, in convivial company, he might become ribald.

Tea was brought in and Aunt Bertha, who was clad in what Julia called 'Biblical Purple,' presided with the pompousness of one performing familiar rites. I felt she was hostile to us all although, to do her justice, she tried valiantly to make herself agreeable. I knew Emmy, who sat beside her, was disliking her intensely and she in her turn was not drawn to this aloof girl whom she longed to patronise but could not. I could tell, however, from the manner in which her attention constantly strayed to where Julia sat, that it was with my elder sister she was chiefly concerned. Julia had been papa's most constant companion and ever since she had been small he had been accustomed to treat her as though she were his contemporary. At home we all took her power of conversation for granted, but that afternoon I saw Christine's two brothers looked admiring yet askance as she sat disputing most charmingly with their father. As for Aunt Bertha, she was suspicious, on principle, of Julia's charm, for she belonged to that school which considered only the disagreeable could be sincere.

After tea we went outside and saw enough of the gardens, sloping to the south within high walls, to visualise how beautiful they would be in mid-summer. The gardens and well-kept lawns clustered round the house. Beyond them the ground was uncultivated, as though the gardeners had grown discouraged and been content to plant rhododendron bushes on either side of the avenue to screen from view the barren land which gave the place an uninhabited appearance.

They asked us if we would care to play a game of croquet; this would be the first time they had played this year, they told us. Edwin Strathern partnered Julia and I was coupled with Nicholas. He was rather quelling to look at and I expected him to be impatient or angry if I played a poor shot and felt inordinately grateful when I found he was neither. Emmy played with Martin, whose eye glittered when it fell on her, as it always did when it rested on any pretty thing.

We were all laughing and Emmy was clapping her hands when I noticed, striding towards us, a tall young man, his fair hair shining yellow in the sun. Christine dropped her mallet when she saw him and ran over the lawn.

'Why, Stephen,' she said reproachfully, 'you never told me you were coming to-day. The Misses Lockhart met you at my ball, didn't they? This is their youngest sister, Miss Lisbet. And now you must come and partner me, for I am being disgracefully beaten.'

He joined in the game and play grew most exciting. Julia was very poor at it and a serious handicap to Mr Strathern, but Emmy was winning until Stephen Wingate suddenly knocked her ball out of bounds.

It was a day in late spring and we all sat round the table at our evening meal, while papa's hand beat on the cloth, a sign that he was upset. The letter, handed in by young Malcolm Gow, from the new dominie of Barnfingal school, lay in front of him. It was written in a uniformly sloping hand and was an invitation asking the minister if he would attend a demonstration of the dominie's scholars. Papa, who enjoyed the company of his contemporaries, was uncomfortable with children, but he felt duty-bound to accept the invitation, and, as he always liked his discomforts to be shared, said Julia must accompany him.

'You had better come too,' he remarked, as though recollecting something when his glance fell on me.

'Why, dear?' asked mamma. She had to repeat her question for lately papa had grown somewhat deaf, as though to cut himself off still further from disturbing influences. 'Why do you want Lisbet to go with you and Julia?' she repeated in a slightly louder voice.

'He is a very good Latin scholar, I believe,' papa informed her, 'and I want to arrange for Lisbet to have lessons from him twice a week. It would absorb too much of my time to teach her myself. And she must go to him as he won't be able to charge so much then. The whole morning's going to be most inconvenient. Dominie Naughton never had any of this demonstration nonsense.'

'No, papa,' Julia reminded him, wearying of his impatience, 'and you were always saying the loch trout received more attention from Dominie Naughton than the children ever did.'

Papa performed his duties amongst his dispersed congregation with the undeviating punctiliousness that was characteristic of him, but as the years passed the less he had to do the more disinclined he seemed to do it. He liked each day to pass the same as the one before and became easily irritated when shaken out of his groove. He was learned but had neither the patience nor understanding to make a sympathetic teacher, so that I was relieved when I heard him announce I was to receive my finishing lessons from the dominie.

Neither Emmy nor I had ever very much to say to papa, but Julia, who could read him like a book, never had any difficulty in making him discourse on whatever subject she happened to be interested in. She could not be called studious, but her imagination coloured and her receptive thoughts enlivened what he told her, while her restless questing mind found food amongst his books.

We left the manse about eleven on the morning of the demonstration. By the time we were half-way to Barnfingal, papa, under Julia's influence, was talking with animation about the tribes of ancient Scotland, the 'smeared people' of the far north, the 'hunters' of Galloway, the Caledonians of our own and neighbouring shires, the 'horsemen' of Arygll, and the squat, dark, 'unbekent' people found sometimes in the Hebrides who are believed to be either relics of the Lost Ten Tribes or descendants of sailors wrecked from the Spanish Armada.

Barnfingal was two miles from the manse and one came upon it suddenly, with its few white-washed, thatched cottages scattered up the hillside and its graveyard walled in by a round, low, grass-topped dyke and warded by the gable-end of a ruined church.

When we reached the crest of the steep winding brae leading into it, the smoke from the straw chimneys was the only visible sign of life. Otherwise one might have imagined that some terrible scourge had made an end to all the inhabitants and no one had come near the clachan since from a superstitious dread.

Green hill rising behind green hill—they raised in me

a brooding, inherent melancholy. I felt this place had lived
through everything, had seen everything, that it was saturated with memories and legends. I thought of it submerged
under the sea, of the ocean receding farther and farther
from it; of glaciers creeping down the mountains, forming
the glens and ravines; of the mountains as spent volcanoes
covered by the impenetrable Caledonian forest. And now
there was nothing more for it to know and it was waiting
for the clap of doom.

The schoolhouse stood back from the road, its three-
cornered playground surrounded by ploughed fields as
though they would fain encroach upon it. When we arrived
at the gate, we heard through the wide-open door the loud
chattering of children, but as we walked across the playground, a sudden silence fell, as if the noise had dropped
through the floor.

The dominie came forward to greet us. His broad shoulders wore a deprecating stoop as though apologising for his
height, and he spoke in the slow, concentrated English of
a Gaelic speaker. His low voice had a curious effect on
his listeners. It was like a voice heard in lonely, echoing
places; his words seemed to linger in the air long after he
had spoken, as a twig still trembles when the bird has flown.

There was something almost foreign in his appearance
as he stood with his head to one side while he listened,
smilingly attentive, to what papa had to say. It was some
minutes before I traced this strangeness to his eyes and
discovered that, while one was blue, the other was brown.
This peculiarity lent him an unfamiliar look, as though he
were some one from a different planet, or as though each of
his eyes looked out on a different world.

The children rose to their feet when we entered and the
dominie brought forward a chair for me. Evidently he had
expected papa to bring one of us with him, for beside his
desk, adorned with flowers and ferns, where the minister
was to sit, stood a chair for Julia which had been made
into a bower. Armfuls of flowers and ferns were arranged
round the room and some drawings of birds and insects had

been pinned to the blackboard beside a few lined maps, with herring-bone mountain ranges and eel-like rivers.

A vast dumbness had spread over the children, who watched our every movement, all except little Jinty MacPhee, the mole-catcher's daughter, and her gaze was fixed to her drawing of a thrush on the blackboard as though she expected it to fly away. There were about a score sitting on the whittled forms before us, the girls with red buttons of noses and blunt mouths, the boys with their large knuckled hands, big knees and swinging, scratched bare legs.

The proceedings began with their singing several songs in unison, then Ian Malloch, at the dominie's prompting, rose to give a short recitation. His voice came and went huskily, but he kept on until the end, while his elder sister Maggie, knotting her fingers together in her nervousness, leant forward on the bench and watched his face intently as she frantically lipped his words. The five members of the Gow family now delivered with gusto and appropriate gestures 'The Bonnie House o' Airlie'. They were all red-haired and had the same jutting-out underlip—Nannie was wont to say that 'gash-gabbit' children were usually forward and 'quick on the uptak''.

*Ten bonny sons I have borne unto him,*
   *The eleventh ne'er saw his daddy;*
*Although I had a hundred more,*
   *I would give them all to Prince Charly,*

they finished triumphantly. After them, the three smallest girls sang in high sweet voices a quaint little song about rocking a baby to sleep.

'They're some verses sung often in the parts from where I come, Miss Lockhart,' the dominie announced suddenly, addressing Julia as though she had spoken. He stood behind me and as I listened to his voice I wondered from where it was he came. 'If you should so desire it, I can write out the lines for you.'

Julia thanked him and declared they were so pretty she would indeed like to have them. More songs were sung and recitations delivered. I think the dominie hoped the minister would now examine some of the older boys, but papa made no such proposal; indeed he appeared anxious to be gone. Perhaps the dominie sensed the preoccupied tenseness which sometimes emanated from him, as though he had been interrupted in the midst of something vitally important; anyway he went with us most readily to the door and accompanied us across the playground. I thought papa had forgotten about my lessons and was swallowing my disappointment, but at the gate he turned to the dominie and said:

'Mr MacDonald, I want to arrange with you to teach my youngest daughter Latin. I propose that you give her two lessons a week, on Tuesdays and Fridays, and that she comes to you in the afternoon, when she would not impinge upon your other lessons. She could perhaps begin this coming Tuesday?'

'Yes,' Julia said suddenly, 'Tuesday would be quite suitable.'

We left the dominie looking after us with his disconcerting eyes, one of his hands still holding open the gate through which we had passed.

Julia had a headache; at least it was not actually a headache but a feeling of torpor, caused probably by the thundery weather. Emily said she knew the sensation exactly. 'You feel,' she sympathised, 'like a cottage that has a heavy fall of snow on its thatch.' Julia said she could not bear to remain in the house, so would come with me for my first lesson from the dominie and perhaps the walk would do her good. Emmy would not accompany us; the next worse thing to being taught Latin yourself, she said, was hearing some one else taught it. She would stay at home and help mamma stitch the new braid on to her old tunic, but she came with us as far as the manse gate which opened on to the road.

Sound took long to carry on the air burdened with the heavy, sweet smells that herald a thunder-storm. A faint mist had crept amongst the trees, filling up the spaces between the branches, so that they looked like spectral things. Shadows dragged on the loch, the mountains bulked forebodingly near, heat smote down from the low sky, and mist unrolled like dust from under the feet of a vast invisible army. Everything looked dead and ghostly, only the human beings were real, alive inhabitants of a dream world—Emmy bidding us good-bye, Julia with her high cheek-bones set well apart, broadening her face, the carter's boy whistling beside his steaming horse.

We set off briskly along the road towards Barnfingal. I took off my bonnet and felt the sun hot upon the nape of my neck. The darkened landscape was like an old Biblical print in one of papa's books at home, for the rays of the sun shot down obliquely from behind accumulating clouds, and it was raining in a slanting sheet on the other side of the loch.

We met the Gow Farm children on the brae coming home from school, so knew we were not late. The dominie was waiting for us, with several books he had looked out to discover which was the most suitable for me. I had always taken a delight in Latin and, even when I was quite small, loved translating the simplest sentences. Balbus who built a wall, the humble queen who washed the feet of the sailors, the nameless explorer who set out on a journey, all became personalities to me, and even the bald statement that ground is arable filled me with pleasure. I enjoyed my lesson from the dominie, who was a patient and encouraging teacher, and who secretly gratified me by saying I was further on than he had expected.

While he sat beside me, Julia moved about the school-room, reading the initials carved on the benches and looking at the slates piled on the dominie's desk. My lesson lasted an hour and by the end of that time she was quite ready to be talkative. For want of something better to do she had taken a yellow flower out of a jar and was blowing its tight little buds open.

'Tell me, Mr MacDonald,' she asked, her lips curving into her bewitching smile, 'I have been wondering so much as I listened to your voice from where you come.'

'My mother came from the Nordeneys,' he answered as he rose and shut his books. 'That's a far cry from here. And my father was a native of Mhorben.'

'He's dead then?'

'They're both dead—my mother died at my birth and my father some years ago.'

She stood looking up into his face.

'I feel you were an only child,' she said, 'and were brought up by your "lone self", not in the rough and tumble of a large family.' She was merely speaking her thoughts, for we all conjectured and made up stories about the people we met.

He smiled and shook his head at her.

'I was the seventh,' he said.

'And your father,' she questioned instantly, 'was he a seventh child too?'

'Yes,' he replied uneasily. 'Why do you ask that?'

'Ah,' Julia exclaimed triumphantly, 'then you will have second sight. What is it Nannie calls it again?—"the vision of the two worlds".'

He was palpably taken aback and repudiated it hurriedly.

'But, Mr MacDonald,' she insisted, 'a curious thing happened when we were here the other day. You answered a question of mine before I asked it.'

'Did I?' he replied, perplexed. 'I did not notice, I do not recollect. But that is not the second sight.'

'Perhaps not, but you read thoughts?'

'Sometimes I can,' he admitted reluctantly.

There was a pause and then Julia said, 'That must make you feel very powerful,' and I saw her colour deepen.

'I would give much not to be able to do it,' he said, and he spoke so strenuously for so tranquil a person that I was startled.

'Why?' Julia challenged. In an effort to be at ease again, she began to speak rapidly. 'I would have imagined it would put you in such a strong position—for one thing you will never be surprised at anything you hear and will always be prepared. What does it feel like to read people's thoughts?'

'I don't read them,' he said, 'I see them.'

'See them!' And when he did not explain, she pressed, 'How do you mean "see them"?'

'They come and go before my eyes in pictures.'

I thought it unfair to question one who was so obviously unwilling to answer, but nothing would stay Julia.

'How strange,' she remarked. 'And when you are with several people, what happens then?'

'Then their thoughts behave mostly like cows all running in wrong directions.'

'I see,' Julia said; 'now I know why you don't like reading them,' and her smile looked somehow twisted. 'You must feel as though you were walking through people. I would have imagined it would be an advantage, not a drawback; that it would have given you a start in life, added something to it.'

'I think this life is given us to find out how much we can do without.'

'Nonsense,' she rallied, her old self once again, 'we are here to enjoy, to have and to share, not to deny and chill ourselves.'

He did not contradict her but I was aware that he had withdrawn himself from us. He was taller than she and had to gaze down into her eyes which were darkened by the brim of her tilted hat. He was not cadaverous, but his features were those that threw shades on his face. I noticed there were shadows in the pits where his eyes were, in the dent of his chin and the concaves of his nostrils.

For the best part of a week we had not been able to leave the house and had spent the days hung with rain alone in the manse with mamma, papa and Nannie, visited only by the irregular mail.

Two unfortunate things happened during that time. Julia had won a playful wager with Edwin Strathern, who handsomely paid it by sending her six pairs of gloves. When they arrived, however, she found they were not large enough, for, in a fit of quite unusual vanity, she had told him a size smaller than she really took. She despatched them back to the shop which paid no attention either to the returned gloves or her letter asking for them to be exchanged. 'And they would have done so beautifully for me,' mourned Emmy.

She had made so ambitious a twirl design in the corners of mamma's tunic that half-way round she discovered she was not going to have nearly enough braid to finish. More material had to be written for and mamma said the tunic was working out much dearer than it was worth.

The patter of rain on the skylights, the drippings from the trees outside, were a ceaseless accompaniment throughout the days and nights. The rain-streaked windows darkened the already dark house. In the bedrooms the massive dressing-tables were placed at the windows, blocking the little light that managed to slip between the branches of the trees. The long rolls made out of padded blue cloth, now faded to a hyacinth purple, which lay along the window-sills to dry up any damp, were wet when we turned them each morning.

33

Emmy grew restless and Julia, as the mist stole nearer and nearer the manse, became more remote and silent and inaccessible, as though wrapt in another world. She had received a letter from the dominie, enclosing the verses of the lullaby she liked. I was untutored in the ways of men but I knew he had pretended to forget to give her them on Tuesday that he could have an excuse to write.

I was troubled at the rain because it prevented my walking to Barnfingal on Friday for my lesson. Julia wanted me to go despite it, and said she would come with me, but as the steady downpour made no signs of abatement, mamma would not hear of it and asked Julia what she could be thinking of.

At last, late on the Saturday afternoon, the rain began to lessen. Light broke palely from the reaches of sky, then the sun burst through gloriously, like a guest who knows well his visit is long overdue. We ate supper hurriedly, so anxious were we to be out, and even Emmy, after we had finished, was ready quickly. She might be going only as far as the manse gate, but always she dressed herself as carefully as though she were bound to meet the Laird.

The mud sucked at our shoes as we ran, laughing, up the path, through the wood, with its glistening wet trees, to the gate where raindrops swung from the bars. We were all feeling a little fey after being confined for so long to the house. Julia was singing 'Caller Herrin'' in a pensive voice, as though experimenting with her notes and the clear, cool air, Emmy had her hands full of dripping red mosses she intended to plant in the garden because she liked their colour, and I had on a very old straw hat with a broken cone-shaped crown and must have looked wild for I felt my hair pushing through it. We were walking towards Barnfingal—Julia said she liked it better than Auchendee—and had reached the sand-pit, with its exposed knotted roots of trees, when Emmy said suddenly:

'Who's that over there?'

'Where?' asked Julia, looking round. 'Oh, why, that must be Mr MacDonald, the dominie.'

He was standing with his back towards us, beside a tree some yards from the road, watching something so intently that he did not hear us.

'Let's go and see what he's looking at,' Julia proposed.

Emmy was as interested as she and we crossed the sodden grass. He looked round sharply at our approach and his eyes lit up as he recognised us. Now that we were beside him, we saw that what he had been looking at with such absorption was a gipsy encampment in a small clearing amongst the trees. There were three or four tents, all dirty and so low they could hardly be dignified by the name of tent. They were sopping wet and every now and then flapped heavily, with a sound like a slap, in the slight breeze. A cart rested on its shafts and beside it grazed a tethered, lean-flanked horse.

'There's something happened here,' the dominie said in a lowered voice, 'but I can't make out what it is. No one seems to be about.'

'There's some one in there,' said Emmy, pointing to the largest of the tents.

From underneath the flap a fierce little child looked out, watching us blackly. I could not have told whether it were male or female, for it had the face of a boy but was dressed in tattered skirts. Julia advanced towards it and spoke to it softly but it would answer her nothing.

Suddenly we were surrounded by a group of staring children of varying ages and sizes. So quickly did they appear around us that they seemed to have sprung from the ground like enchanted mushrooms.

'Where are all your fathers and mothers?' Julia asked them laughingly.

They gathered round us closer. 'They' were burying Hester's boy, they told us and their dark eyes watched us fearfully as though the properties of life and death lay in our hands. He had died last night. 'They' had asked several of the crofters' wives to come and see him to tell them what was the matter with him, but none of them would come. We were not surprised, for well we knew the fear with which the crofters and farmers regarded those dusky aliens who kept to themselves with the aloofness of royalty. The pig-wife who came round every year with her heavy burden of china was sure of a seat and something to eat in any of the cottages, the gangrel tinkers who mended pots and pans were always asked for news, as were the other itinerants who walked over the hills peddling tapes and buttons from village to clachan. But gipsies were a different race altogether from tinkers and tramps.

'We had better go,' said Emmy.

The dominie gave Julia a coin which she slipped into the palm of the little lowering gipsy, but he was not expecting it and let it fall from his hand.

'He is like a little fate,' she said, looking down at him wistfully.

'A little fate that won't be bribed,' smiled the dominie.

We were turning away when I felt Emmy's hand on my arm.

'There,' she whispered, 'they're coming back.'

We stood close to the tree, at some distance from the tents, and watched. A silent, secretive procession was returning to the encampment. A rough-haired pony, drawing an empty cart, was followed by the gipsies in an uneven file. I knew that the cart's last burden had been the boy's dead body. They had buried him somewhere and his relations had followed him to his grave in strict precedence of next of kin. They would have buried his stick with him so that it could be of aid to him in the next world. Poor gipsy boy! We watched them move about the encampment, burning the tent in which he had lain and with it all his few belongings. Then we saw them gather their things together, harness the lean horse, and depart.

'I recognised those gipsies,' Emmy said as we walked back to the road, 'they come round every year with the May-gobs' (cold weather about the second week of May).

'They won't return,' the dominie told her, 'for gipsies never camp again where one of them has died.'

We stood talking with him for some ten minutes before we went on our different ways. He was the only person I have ever met who was able to smile with his eyes while his lips remained grave; I think that was what gave him so kindly an expression and led people to confide in him. He looked smilingly from one to the other of us now, as though he were so glad he had met us, tracing resemblances and differences in our three faces.

'Do you like him?' Julia asked anxiously when we had turned the corner.

'He's very nice,' Emmy murmured indifferently; 'he looks an ideal dominie from the children's point of view.'

'Papa says,' Julia said, almost resentfully, 'that he was one of the most brilliant scholars of his year at Glasgow College. He won everything he could for mathematics.'

'I wonder what he's doing buried up here then,' observed Emmy; 'that's Highland, of course. Yes, he's very nice, but a little like a moral come alive—no matter what you said or did to him, it would never alter his negative course. Isn't it funny?—now I come to think of it, we have never seen him in church. Let's go and visit some one to-night, I don't feel I want to go home for hours and hours yet. I wish the Stratherns were back. Not that we could visit them to-night even if they were, but they do add an excitement.'

'The only person we can visit is old Mrs Wands, and you know how difficult it is to get away from her.'

'But let's go and see her all the same,' insisted Emmy; 'it's weeks since we've been.'

We were always sure of finding Mrs Wands at home, for she was bed-fast. When we tapped on the door it was opened as though by magic, for no one stood behind it. The old woman, who was the ferryman's mother, had a rope attached to the latch and, when any one 'chapped,' she pulled the rope from her bed.

I used to be afraid of her when I was small and she had been able to move about her overgrown garden. In those days she had worn a man's cap with a hat-pin thrust through

38

it like a skewer, and after we had had a meal with her she had let the hens into the kitchen to pick up the crumbs. Now she lay very still in the cupboard bed, her mouth puckered round her gums and her voice like the wind whistling through reeds. Her eyes were bright with the brightness one sees only in the very old or the very young, and her face was rutted and tracked, as though she had once wept a lot and the tears had made inroads on her cheeks. She was always so glad to see us it made us feel grieved with ourselves we had not visited her oftener.

'Find seats for yoursels,' she told us, after her greeting. 'Ach, Miss Lisbet, ye always gang to the settle—ye're so quiet ye mak' folk forget aboot ye. Ye're growing, Miss Emmy, but ye're no going to be near as tall as your sister.'

'She's very glad of that,' Julia said, 'for now there's such a difference between us she can't wear my old clothes.'

'Noo, Miss Emmy, ye ken where to find the tea. Swing the kettle on to the swee and it will no be mair than twa-three minutes afore it's through the boil. And, Miss Lisbet, ye'll find the oatcakes in yon tin at the end o' the dresser and a platter to put them on. And so, Miss Julia, your faether's buried ma gentle friend Katie MacPhee. Did he tell ye wha held the cords? Aweel, ne'er heed; Dookit is ferrying Ian MacPhee o'er the loch the nicht and will hear it frae him. She thocht she was going, puir soul, for no so lang afore she changed a queer thing happened to her. She always wore twa pair o' spectacles, ye mind, and she was reading the Bible one evening as she had done for the last twelve year. She was a gey slow reader and had only reached Leviticus. She was reading awa' when she took aff one pair o' spectacles and then the second pair, and there she saw the print big and clear afore her een as though she was a bairn again and had hardly used her sicht. "Ah me," she plained to Jinty, "I've got ma second sicht." And within a week they had kisted her.'

'Mrs Wands,' said Julia, 'have you ever met any one who had the other kind of second sight? I don't mean the second sight some have just before death, but the second sight

that is born in some people, that makes them see into the
future and able to foretell what is to befall. There are
people who have it very strongly, aren't there?'

'There are some wha have their doors and windows
opened wider than ithers,' the old woman replied guardedly,
'and then some things are bound to come ben to them, and
there are ithers wha's clocks always gang a wee thing fast.
But whate'er happens to ye, it's God's will and happens for
the best.'

As I sat at the fire and watched the tiny pieces of ash
dancing on the black kettle and the heated resin wetting
the burning logs, I wondered if one had to live to be nearing
eighty before one could believe that.

'The new dominie noo—' she pursued, pulling herself
up to a sitting posture with the help of a piece of rope which
dangled from the ceiling for that purpose, and putting out
shaking hands for the cup Emmy was holding for her.

'Yes, the new dominie?' Julia interrogated eagerly.

'He was ben here on Tuesday—he comes sometimes
to see hoo I am when Dookit's kept on the ither side o' the
loch, but on Tuesday he had come to borrow a piece o'
candle frae me. That was Katie MacPhee's burial day, ye
mind, and as he was making up the fire for me, he fell to
talking aboot sickness and pain and sudden death. "Ay,
ay, Mistress Wands," he says to me, "when ye learn whit
graund things ye can do wi' figures, ye canna doot that God
can do whit He wills wi' souls." Yon was a queer thing for
the likes o' him to say, for ye ken whit's wrang wi' him?'

'No—what?' we asked, and all drew a little closer.

'I'm no telling any one for I like him weel enow and I ken
there are some here wha would ne'er rest until they were rid
o' him if they kent aboot him.'

'What is it?' questioned Julia.

'Weel, he's a Roman Catholic.'

'Oh.'

'Ay, and when Dookit came hame that day I tauld him the
dominie mayhap would want the candle to say his prayers
by, but next morning he gave it back wi' scarce ony o' it

burnt, so I said to Dookit that his prayers couldna have been o'er lang that nicht. He walks into Dormay every Sabbath and the folk here think he gangs to Mr Urquhart's kirk wi' its kistfu' o' whistles—weel we a' ken your faether would ne'er thole such goings-on in his kirk, Miss Julia. But Dookit once met him on the Dormay brig juist aifter he had come. "Ye're on the wrang road for the kirk, Mr MacDonald," he said to him. "It's no the kirk I'm bound for," he replied, ootspoken as though it was, "it's the chapel at Inverlui."'

'There are many good Roman Catholics,' pondered Julia.

'Mebbe, mebbe, Miss Julia, but aifter Dookit tauld me aboot him yon Sabbath, I always feel there's something hid aboot him, e'en though he hauds your een when he talks to ye. He's unbekent—na like ither folk. And it's no as though he cam' o' Roman Catholic stock, for his faether was an elder in the kirk at Mhorben and passed roond the box every Sabbath.' She lowered her voice. 'But Dookit's foond oot his graundmither was a Roman Catholic afore she married on his graundfaether, but no whit ye could ca' a guid Catholic for she went to the kirk aifter she was marrit. She cam' frae one o' the islands where they think Hallowe'en is the first day o' the new year and heathenish things like yon. Ye're na going? Dinna gang yet—it's guid to hear your voices. Aweel, aweel. Ay, come ben the next time ye're passing. I hear your footfa's and Miss Lisbet's every Tuesday and Friday when she gangs for her lesson. Did ye see the byre's been thatched a' o'er again?'

'Yes, we noticed that,' said Julia, 'and it's looking so tidy and new.'

'Eh. Put your heids in when you're passing—Dookit highered the roof, for the coo was aye catching her horns in it.'

We peered in at the byre which was built on to the gable-end of the low-browed cottage. A white cow glimmered through the darkness that smelt of milk and hay. Its chain clanked as it turned its heavy head to look at us. Through a tiny uneven window, light struggled faintly and lit up a spider's web spanning encrusted beams.

'It's beautiful, Mrs Wands,' Julia went back to tell her, 'and he's made a window too, hasn't he?'

Her veined wrinkled hand was smoothing the bedclothes.

'Ay, ay,' she answered, 'he thocht it wouldna be so dull-like for the coo if she could get a keek oot in the winter.'

# Book Two

Summer thickened the trees, beat in the warming earth, hummed on the wing of bee and dragonfly, and swelled the birds' clamorous song. And with the summer came the Stratherns who returned, as they did every year, to spend several months in their country home.

I had gone to have my lessons from the dominie for some weeks, so that now they had become part of my usual life. Julia sometimes accompanied me and would sit listening to the little summer wind that mourned round the low building while the dominie sat beside me, prompting and correcting. The faded map of Africa looked down on us, flies buzzed drowsily at the window-pane, and the faraway crow of a cock or low of a cow grazing on a distant hill would be borne in on the still air.

One afternoon in August when we returned from Barnfingal we found Emmy had washed her hair and was sitting, a towel over her shoulders, with her back to the parlour fire, for even in summer mamma had to have a fire. Emmy had not Julia's long dark hair, hers scarcely fell beyond her shoulders, but was so fine it shone like silk in the firelight. She had newly brushed it and it sprang, crackling, round her face; each hair seemed to have a separate life of its own and waved about like a thread seeking the eye of a needle.

'I've been thinking, Julia,' she said when we came in, 'that we should give our picnic soon.'

Julia took off her hat and, still holding it in her hand, sat down on the sofa.

'Oh, Emmy,' she asked in a voice that almost entreated, 'do you think we should give it?'

'Of course I do,' Emmy said indignantly; 'it's the smallest thing we could do in return for all the Stratherns' goodness to us. Why, it was you who suggested it.'

'Yes, yes, I know, but that was in winter when summer seemed so distant. Now the thought of it fatigues me; all the preparations and planning, trysting the ferryman to take us there, Nannie in a speechless ferment baking for it, and then, after all, it will probably be wet.'

'We will tell them it's a picnic and not to come if it's wet. You know Nannie loves baking and Lisbet and I can tryst the ferryman if you are as exhausted as all that. Now, whom shall we ask? Christine, of course, and the father and Nicholas and Martin.'

'Martin always makes me feel so arch. Yes, we'll have to ask them all,' sighed Julia.

'But not Aunt Bertha. I refuse to go on a picnic with Aunt Bertha.'

'We'll have to ask her,' said Julia, suddenly laughing, 'but she won't come—I can vouch for that.'

'And who else?' questioned Emmy, her hand stroking her hair on one side while she brushed it on the other.

'There's no one else,' said Julia.

'What about Stephen Wingate?'

'Oh, yes, I quite forgot about him—he's arriving next week, of course. We had better have him too or the day will be spoiled for Christine. We'll have to mix the sets or there won't be enough china to go round.'

We planned the picnic to take place a week on Thursday and engaged the ferryman for the whole of that day. He was very strong, but so thin his skin merely webbed his bones; it was as though he had hollowed himself with so much rowing. I felt even after life had left him his hands would still work automatically with the oars and no one would notice he was dead.

He rowed us over to the little island in the morning, and we set out the china on the cloth, turning the cups upside down in case anything fell into them, and building a fire to boil the kettle on. It all looked very pretty after we had

finished, with posies covering the stones at each corner of
the cloth, and flowers and leaves and ferns twining amongst
the dishes. Above, the foliage of the silver birches swam
more than blew in the gentle breeze, like trees seen in
water.

They arrived about three that afternoon and mamma and
papa came to the loch's edge to see us into the boat. I
trailed my hand through the cool water, while Julia sat in
the stern and Christine in the prow with her arm round
Emmy's waist. They were all in the highest, most festive spirits, particularly Edwin Strathern, who was almost
excited, speaking more than any one and so quickly that
his words must have outpaced his thoughts. He insisted
on taking an oar and rowed so vigorously that Stephen
Wingate and Duguid Wands had trouble to keep in stroke
with him.

Mamma's and papa's pleasant voices thinned into the distance and they dwindled rapidly from view until the trees
behind them seemed to swoop to the loch's edge and hide
them altogether. As we moved farther and farther from
shore, with all its familiar rustlings, flutterings and bestir-
rings, we seemed to float into another land where sound
drifted, light rippled and time glided.

The boat grated on the ground when we neared the
island; Nicholas helped us to disembark and to light the
fire on which to boil the kettle.

'You must excuse our harlequin china,' Julia smiled as she
began to pour out tea.

'It's all beautiful,' said Edwin Strathern, 'it's a fairy
feast—I feel we ought to have wings and sit on toadstools
before we are allowed to partake of it.'

Stephen Wingate's glance lighted on Martin's portly figure and his lips twitched.

'You would think of that, Wingate,' Martin observed
witheringly. He stood back on a twig and nearly capsized.
We all laughed most unkindly. 'I nearly killed myself,' he
remarked gravely; 'what would you have said to that, Miss
Emmy?'

'They would find me with a hairpin through my heart,' she promised him.

I saw Stephen Wingate's blue eyes turn to and dwell on her as she spoke. She was leaning forward, her pink dress dappled by the shadows of the trees above, but no shade fell on her uplifted face. Her eyebrows were slightly raised on each temple, which gave her face a winged, uncommon look. He opened his mouth as if to speak, and I did not think somehow that it was going to be anything particularly pleasant, but evidently he thought better of it for he remained silent.

I sat beside the tall watchful Nicholas. Already I was conscious in an overwhelming degree of his presence. I longed to be brilliant like Julia or unconsciously provocative like Emmy, neither of whom ever had to hesitate for an answer. But I could only punctuate his conversation with monosyllables, feeling very stupid and that he must think so too.

Edwin Strathern began to make up a bouquet of wild flowers for Julia, to say to her, he declared, what he dared not say himself, but he found the island lacking in all the flowers he most wanted.

'I would need a garden all to myself where spring and autumn, summer and winter flowers grow at one and the same time,' he said. 'You know, this is rather a sad little island although it is so sunshiny, for the only things that seem to grow here are forget-me-not, and the spruce fir, which means farewell.'

'And the dandelion, which says depart,' laughed Emmy.

It was then I saw Stephen Wingate stoop and present her with a spray of spiderwort twisted round a sprig of broom, and I heard him say to her with exaggerated concern in his lowered voice, 'I'm so sorry, there should be some parsley amongst it.' I do not think any one else noticed, but I watched what she would do with her 'flower-letter' which I knew was supposed to read ironically, 'Your humility has won my esteem.' She did not even glance round at him but sat looking at the two sprigs in her hand as though she wondered how they had come there; then she threw the spiderwort away, twirled the broom between her finger and thumb as if she did not know what to do with it, smelt it and let it follow the spiderwort over her left shoulder.

We spent a long time over the picnic, and after we had eaten we went to the other side of the tiny island where a ghostly echo lived, and let it play with our voices. Edwin Strathern's deep challenge came floating back to him over the water thin and wailing, Julia's low voice returned full of merriment, Emmy's glad tones startled us by echoing back sad and haunting, and Christine's voice, which had little timbre, broke into pieces in the air, like an hysterical woman's laughter.

Afterwards Edwin Strathern took Julia out in the boat. The rippleless loch, merging from silver to grey and from grey to blue, glittered in the sun like the scales of a fish. I became dazzled looking after them and shut my eyes, only to see bright silver lights, shooting like comets behind my closed lids.

When I opened them again, everything was a little dimmer than I expected, and it was a few seconds before I found the boat. Julia had her head turned away both from us and Edwin Strathern, while he had let one oar slip and was leaning over the other as though beseeching with her.

'She is a sweet pretty little thing,' mamma remarked after they had all gone. 'Of course everything has been done for her.'

'Yes,' Emmy agreed, a little sadly, 'and she has done everything she's wanted—I mean she has done nothing, which is just what she has wanted.'

'When is she to be married?' asked mamma.

'Her father doesn't approve of early marriages and wants her to wait until she is at least eighteen,' replied Emmy.

'If I were she,' said Julia, 'I would let Stephen do a little of the adoring—she watched every mouthful he took as though it were a miracle to see him swallow.'

'They are all nice, the father in particular,' mamma pronounced, veering the conversation round to what she wanted to discuss, 'but the picnic must have tired him, for he was so quiet and flat after it compared to what he was when you all set out. You shouldn't have allowed him to row.'

'Nonsense, mamma,' Emmy exclaimed heatedly, 'that man is far more active than either of his sons. We can't start treating him as though he were bordering on senility.'

Mamma glanced up as Julia suddenly rose and left the room.

'You know, Emmy,' she pursued placidly, 'you must begin to talk more when you are in company. You left the conversation entirely with Julia.'

'But one is much more popular, mamma,' Emmy informed her, 'if one does all the listening and lets one's company do the talking, particularly if the company is male.'

'I saw the eldest son so like his father,' said mamma, 'but I never tell relations they are like each other as I notice they

50

never seem to take it as a compliment. What a pity the Martin one is so stout, for it's not as though he had the pronounced type of features that can command stoutness.'

'When he laughs,' said Emmy, 'he looks so like the Toby jar on the mantelpiece that Nannie keeps her tapers in.'

'Did they make any arrangement when you were to meet them again?' mamma asked with interest.

Emmy was standing at the window, her opened hand pressed against the pane. She lifted it and watched the five-fingered blur it had made contract into nothingness.

'No,' she said, without looking round, 'they didn't.'

'They'll write probably,' conjectured mamma, holding her work away from her that she might see it the better.

But when Christine wrote it was to tell her dearest Emmy that they were leaving for abroad within a week and this was only the merest note to bid good-bye to her and her own dear Juley.

Mamma was upset at their premature departure. 'It seems such a pity,' she confided, sighing, to me, 'when they were all agreeing so amiably together. I hope whenever a man begins to show an interest in Julia, she is not going to chill simultaneously. I was so like that,' she said more brightly, as though warmed at the glowing memory of herself years ago. 'I am sure I noticed your father long before he noticed me—it was at the Allardyces', I remember. And I thought what a nice straight nose that young man has. When he grew really interested in me, I felt my interest in him cooling, until he became desperate, and then I didn't see how I could very well refuse him. He was always asked to people's houses, you know, for he used to be such good company and full of verve. I did really think, if I married him, he would give me all my own way. But I can remember him warning me the night before our wedding that manse mice were even poorer than their church brothers. Strange, the mistakes you make, and if you had your life to live all over again, you would make them just the same. But Julia seemed not to want to meet the Stratherns this time, just when I was beginning to wonder which was the particular one, and it's not as though she could possibly have met any one else.'

The weeks that followed passed dully for Emmy and me, perhaps because we had been unsettled by the excitement the Stratherns always brought with them, and Julia was so bound by her own thoughts to be uncompanionable. Sometimes she would not hear us when we spoke to her, and if she answered it was as though she had had to bring herself back to us from afar. 'Never fall in love,' she said darkly to me, and one morning I heard her, with uncharacteristic sharpness, tell Emmy, who was making her bed, to stop singing, 'If that one ship went down at sea, The poorest soul on earth I'd be.'

She seemed to have great difficulty in making up her mind whether or not she would accompany me when I went to have my Latin lesson, and usually she came when she had stated she would stay at home, and remained when she had said most decidedly she would be coming. After my lessons, the dominie went with us first to the end of the playground, then to the ferryman's cottage, then to the little knoll, until finally he walked with us the two miles to the manse gate.

When we had said good-bye, Julia would take my hand and run between the trees. If a golden leaf fell on us, she would tell me that meant a happy hour, and start to sing at the top of her voice as though it had come already. When a hay-cart came towards us along the road, we would stand aside to let it pass and wish. Julia, whose desires were always so intense they were fraught with anxiety, would cover her eyes with her hands and I would see her lips moving as she wished, as though in prayer.

I could not have told when it was that I became aware in the schoolroom at Barnfingal of looks that met and glances that quickly fell, of sentences half begun and words that were never spoken. No longer was Julia troubled whether or not she should go to the schoolhouse, but set out joyfully with me each Tuesday and Friday to be greeted by him at the door with brightening eyes.

One Tuesday in late autumn she was not able to accompany me as usual, for Mr Urquhart's brother Charles was home from abroad and had come to visit us. Julia primed me to tell the dominie that friends had called but told me not to mention whom they were. He, however, had evidently been watching me coming down the brae alone, for he greeted me with the words, spoken with some excitement:

'Your sister has not been able to come. Would it trouble you to wait after your lesson while I wrote her a letter? You remember, she once told us she wanted to see the place where the Romans are said to have camped? I wondered if she would like me to show her it on Friday after your lesson.'

I sat beside him whilst he wrote the letter and after he handed it to me I bade him a hurried good-bye for fear he would ask for it back. Rain stung my face but I felt my cheeks glow as I ran most of the way to the manse where, in the dark garden, autumn leaves were sticking amongst the shiny holly bushes. Hiding the letter under my jacket, I started to look for Julia and found her alone in our bedroom. She looked round as I entered.

'You're never back already?' she exclaimed. 'What is that you're hiding below your jacket?'

I had meant to tease her a little but something in her manner forbade it, so I only said gladly:

'A letter from him.'

She told me not to be foolish and to give her it at once. After she had read it, she did not mention what it said, but asked me if he had looked disappointed when he saw she was not with me; and if he had, how disappointed; and what had I said to him.

A rough wind blew on Friday, chasing the clouds across a blue sky and blustering through the topmost branches of the creaking trees. On the road to Barnfingal Julia told me the dominie wanted to show us the Roman encampment that afternoon, but I answered I would go home after my lesson.

'No, no,' she said in alarm, 'they would wonder at home where I was if you returned without me.'

'I'll go so far with you then,' I arranged, 'and wait for you until you return.'

She did not reply and after my lesson the three of us set out, leaving the road when we came to the ferryman's cottage and striking towards the hills. I felt curiously glad and light-hearted that afternoon. Nothing could ever account for those feelings of well-being which filled me with a sense of powerful exhilaration. I felt at one with the gangrel winds, the desultory sunshine and the ground that had once stirred with the roots of trees. It was as though I had once been very happy on a day such as this and now, decades later, when I struggled through the dying bracken which stained the hillsides a bright rust brown, I was warmed by the memory of that long ago, forgotten happiness.

Our footsteps disturbed two grouse which rose, with screaming protests, from the ground at our feet and, on whirring wings, beat themselves into the air. The dominie called them 'heather hens' and told us they always seemed to him to cry out, 'Go back! Go back!' At the foot of a green hill we came to the Barnfingal graveyard where I said I would wait for Julia and be sheltered by the dyke.

I sat for some time on the western side of the dyke, looking over the moor, and stared at the bare ground so long that I saw it veined with deep dark colours, wine red, ruby and prune, drawn to the surface by the sun. Amongst the peat hags were little raised islands with tufts of long grasses sprouting from them, which made me think of fantastic hedgehogs. Grasses, purple when in a mass, bent whispering and sighing before the wind, but I was so protected where I sat that it scarcely fanned my face.

I rose at last and, undoing the piece of frayed rope that tied the gates together, went into the graveyard to look for the place where lay 'the charitable remains' of the Lady of Fingal. The cemetery was raised so that in some parts it over-topped the low dyke and it was built round that Cloutie, who only frequents corners, could not enter. Suicides were interred on the side belonging to the 'black north'. The oldest tombs were horizontal slabs raised on stout, short pillars that had now sunk so far into the earth the slabs were half-buried, while a bright green moss had prettily filled the lettering on the upstanding stones, making them hard to read. Some had skulls and crossbones carved on them, others heads of angels, like the crude drawings of children, some winged hour-glasses, and others fists holding opened books.

My skirts swished in the long grasses, which wetted their hems as I moved from stone to stone over the eardmeal that covered molesmen and elders, shepherds and farmers, their spouses, relicts and children who had 'departed this life'. I loved that expression; there was something gentle and acquiescent about it, as though they had at last found the door they had been seeking all their days.

'. . . And also his spouse Florah Malcolm . . .' I read and gave a little start, for even now voices were lowered when they spoke of Florah, who had been credited with having the Evil Eye. Strange tales they told of her. When crofters, taking their cow home from grazing, had met her, they had been wont to say in passing, 'Good evening, Mistress Malcolm. God bless me and God bless my cow.' But the story that haunted me was the story of the Pedlar Woman and her child.

There were some still living who remembered the day the Pedlar Woman came to Barnfingal. She left her little boy at the mill to play while she went with her wares of bootlaces and gaudy beads to the clachan of Moccoth, higher up the hill. When dusk was thickening into night, old Mrs Stewart, the miller's mother, heard the sound of a child's crying and, going to the door of her cottage, she saw a little boy who said that his mother had never returned.

Late though it was a consultation was held among the crofters that night, for the Pedlar Woman had been seen early in the afternoon on the path to Florah's and there were ugly rumours afloat about the cottage on the old drove road to Balmader. It was said that at different times travellers, walking over the hills and going in to the croft to ask the way or for a drink of milk, were never seen again.

Lots were drawn among the crofters and he who pulled the fated number went to make inquiries at the cottage. It was Florah's daughter who came to the door and, yes, they had seen a pedlar woman that very day but she had gone away, they thought, on the road over the hills; they had not known she had a child, he was not with her when they saw her. The little boy was sent to Perth but the Pedlar Woman was never heard to have reached either Perth or Balmader and was never seen in the district again.

Sometimes people, passing through the long, lush grass warmed by the sun beside the mill, have paused and fancied they heard through the creeping darkness the frightened crying of a child when he finds himself alone.

The fear of her Evil Eye guarded Florah while she was alive. Now her croft was in ruins, and although the unpruned apple trees in her garth still bore fruit, no one ever plucked them. The cottage was built high on the banks of the burn and it was said that the ground between the ruins and the bank could not settle. Each year it slipped a little farther, until in so many years it was supposed to crumble away altogether below the croft and reveal its ghastly secret. There was something malevolent even in her tomb, with its rusted iron railings closing it round, which made me wonder if she too could not settle.

I found the Lady of Fingal's stone and read with ease what was written there, for the gravedigger never allowed it to become obscured with moss or rank grass like the other tombs:

> *If ever virtue gain'd sincere esteem*
> *Or shed a lustre o'er life's fleeting dream*
> *That happy lot was thine in worth approved*
> *Bless'd by the poor by all who knew belov'd*
> *Unstain'd thy life in ev'ry view display'd*
> *Calm reason's power when by Religion sway'd*
> *And now tho' here thy Mortal parts assigned*
> *With spirits bless'd above thy soul is join'd.*

The former gravedigger used to tell, I believe, of how, returning one wild autumn evening to the cemetery for a forgotten spade, he was startled at seeing something white gleam palely through the darkness. Going forward, he discovered that the rowan tree growing on the Lady of Fingal's grave bloomed with creamy blossom that neither shook nor rustled in the high wind tearing round it.

'Life how short, Eternity how long,' bemoaned one stone. 'Whomsoever read the other side,' warned another, 'beware of death for it happened quickly to me on a market day in Dormay.' 'Ian Campbell, Piper to the Marquis of Mhoreneck, died in his twenty-first year,' yet another ran. Then very contentedly I read of one who 'died at Leith but now is buried in this churchyard in peace and with friends and neighbours.'

I liked the rhyming epitaphs best and with my finger picked out the grey lichen and green moss furring some of the stones that I might read their dim, chipped legends. And as I read, it was as though the ghost of him who lay underneath rose from his grave to speak with me. There was something amiable and friendly about Homish MacLean whose confiding epitaph ran:

*This little spot is all my lot*
   *And all that kings acquire;*
*My home's above, a gift of love,*
   *O reader, there aspire.*

Catherine MacDiarmid's read sadly when I pulled aside
the tangle of weeds covering her grave to trace out the
words:

*Troubles sore oft times I bore,*
   *Physicians were in vain;*
*Till God above, in His great love,*
   *Reliev'd me of my pain.*

But I did not care for the one next it, which belonged to a
Duncan Ross who exhorted me almost spitefully to:

*Remember, Man, as you pafs by,*
   *As you are now so once was I,*
*As I am now, so must you be,*
   *Remember, Man, that you must die.*

I thought of Nannie who was wont to say death and the
tax-gatherer were the only two things of which we could be
certain in this uncertain world.

In a less over-crowded part of the graveyard I came upon
a small cross that looked as though it were flying as it stood
on a little hump. Kneeling beside it, I read its story which
plained:

*The/Fairest Flower/that/Decks the sod/*
*must/Close their eyes/To meet/Their/God.*

Suddenly I became aware of the hollow-toned wind, like
the united voice of those who lay buried there, moaning
round the graveyard. I had forgotten to tie up the gate
again with the piece of rope and every now and then it
was blown to by the wind with a dull clang. I looked up
to find myself surrounded by grey crosses and stones pin-
nacled with draped urns. The rustlings at my feet sounded
unaccountable. The gate, at the other side of the cemetery,
looked disproportionately far away.

I began to walk towards it slowly, to show I know not
whom that I was not afraid. But once I stepped outside, I
banged it behind me as though I had reached it only in the

nick of time, and tied it up as quickly as my chilled fingers fumblingly allowed.

I did not look within again, between the railings, in case I would see them, a silent, ghostly company—all whose 'soul sheaths' had been buried there in the graveyard on the hill, Malcolms, Stewarts, MacLeans: the erst-time piper to the Marquis of Mhoreneck, the dew of youth upon his spectral brow; he to whom death had come swiftly that market day in Dormay; Florah with her Evil Eye burning fierily in the middle of her forehead; and, growing from a flowering rowan tree, the Lady of Fingal.

I heard Julia's voice thrilling with laughter, and saw them come towards me. She had taken off her bonnet and the unbridled wind swept through her hair, drawn back from her brow, as she jumped from tussock to tussock, her hand in his. Together we made our way back to the road. The wind tirled in the hollow of my ear and in the west clouds drove like chariots across the setting sun.

At the manse gate they said good-bye to each other in the same way, I suppose, that all lovers bid each other good-bye. Before we turned the bend in the path, something made me glance back at him. He was standing where we had left him, still looking after us, as though bereft.

That was the first of many such meetings; and as the autumn hardened into winter and the afternoons shortened, Julia and I used to meet him each Saturday on the hills behind Barnfingal. She was tall but her head only came up to his shoulder, and he could lift her with ease across burns, swollen with autumn rains.

They would walk together and I would follow or wait for them amongst the ruined sheilings, where I felt invisible things rush past me on the wind. The ground was mazed with old peat tracks, criss-crossing one another, and broken up with bright patches of light green or deep red, spongy sphagnum moss. The loch was lost from view here and, surrounded by the deep-shadowed blue of distant unfamiliar mountains, I felt as one in a remote country.

Was this really only the haunt of the unseen curlew, the plaintive peeweet, the golden plover, the rare northern diver? What went on behind those creeping mists that wreathed the mountain tops or stole along their foot?

Were unseen armies being marshalled behind them, armies that walked on air? Was it from them that sometimes, alone on the hillside, I heard fugitive whispers, bugles blown softly and muffled, caught glimpses of white faces straining through the mist?

The dominie could read from a snail on a blade of grass or the flight of a bird every whim of the weather. He would tell us it was not going to thunder because he had noticed a trout jumping in the loch or that we must expect rain for he had seen a craikie heron 'take to the hill'. There were other things he told us of as he helped us over dykes or went in front to guide us through boggy places: how death and the eddying fairies came from the pale west, and the white chancy south brought summer and long life, giants and ill-luck strode from the black north, and only good could come out of the sacred east.

Sometimes I marvelled that Julia and he had been drawn to one another, for they were so apart in temperament and outlook they might have sprung from two different races. She had never known the calmness and tranquillity bred of unconflicting thoughts. Carried on by the strength of her convictions, she questioned and wrestled with life, tried to force it to yield to her what she wanted; while he accepted, unresisting, whatever came to him. I often wondered if this unquestioning compliance with life simply amounted to letting time solve all problems or was because he walked in step with the future. He so often felt, sensed, saw—I know not in which form his foredooms came to him—what lay in store, that all his days were shadowed by the inevitable. To attempt to evade or change it, he thought as fruitless as attempting to thwart or force the wind. I remember the curious expression of mingled apprehension and sorrow on his face when Julia once said chidingly that he was so sure of defeat he never went into battle.

When the snow came, we could no longer walk with him on the hills and moors. Sometimes it was too wintry for me to attempt the two miles to Barnfingal for my lesson, but each time I went, Julia accompanied me. After my lesson we would sit with him round the schoolroom fire, while hail spat down the chimney and sizzled to extinction in the flames.

Winter tarried long and the heaped mountains withdrew under their covering of snow. I was always the first to be in bed and would lie waiting for Emmy and Julia to come upstairs. As I lay, my eyes wide-open, the house itself seemed to come alive in the darkness in a creaking, alien way: the window would cheep, the door shake as though some one were trying the handle, little noises, like sighs, would sound on the skylight, and surreptitious footsteps crowd past on the landing outside; until I felt cut off from all my fellow creatures and immured by myself in this shell of a house. I always wanted to cry out with relief when I heard Emmy's light step on the stairs and the little quick run she gave as she neared the top. I would sit up in bed under the sloping ceiling, and when Julia came up, the three of us would gossip, while the shadow of their arms waved and wavered on roof and wall.

Spring crept over the hills and at the earth's crust the sky lightened imperceptibly as each day the sun swung a little higher in the heavens. Emmy found the first primrose, growing in the manse wood beside the burn.

'Wrap yoursels up weel,' Nannie told Julia and me, 'for I can tell frae the feel in the wind that it's the Gowk Storm that's boding.'

We were standing in the kitchen before setting off for Barnfingal. Nannie's face was fire-flushed as she stooped over the girdle. It was not her usual baking-day, but Mr Ferguson, the Balmader minister, had come to visit papa, and visitors were as important to Nannie as they were to us. I asked her to give me something to eat before I left and she lifted from the girdle, with hands dusted with flour, a pancake which was so gloriously hot I had to keep changing it from hand to hand as I ate it.

'There is something so unlikely about snow in April,' Julia said pensively, staring out of the little side window.

'Ay,' Nannie conceded, 'juist when the farmers are talking o' sowing and lambing. But it's the unlikely things that always happen in this world.'

'The poor lambs and primroses,' condoled Julia.

'It will pass if they but thole it,' Nannie said summarily, sitting on the creepie with the bellows between her knees and blowing the fire brighter. 'That's whit Gowk Storm means, something o' ill chance that micht fa' to ony o' us and that willna bide. Noo dinna dawdle on the way hame, for I canna think it's juist a lesson that keeps ye so lang every aifternoon ye gang to Barnfingal.'

Fingal was discountenancing on the other side of the loch and storm brooded in the fir trees which stood out, deepened in hue, against the monotonously grey sky. Our footsteps rang on the road and a piercing north wind blew, ranging through the budding trees. It was so bleak I was glad to reach Barnfingal.

The schoolroom was a long low room built on, like an afterthought, to the dominie's house, the only two-storied building, besides Gow's Farm, in Barnfingal. All the previous schoolmasters had possessed a numerous family; and as we crossed the playground that afternoon, it struck me for the first time that our dominie must find his house a little solitary shared only by his shadow. It might have been uninhabited, for nothing could be seen through its four uncurtained windows, against which the light, distorted on the blind glass, flattened itself as though unable to enter.

Julia was restless that afternoon; perhaps Nannie's last words had disturbed her. She kept talking to us while I was having my lesson, so that the dominie, for makeweight, gave me a little longer. When he had done with me, Julia said she would like to go a walk on the hills. He agreed readily enough, although he did say there was snow in the wind; but warnings never meant anything to Julia, and the three of us started off from the schoolroom.

Once on the hills we found the dominie was right, for the wind was so bitter and cold it seemed to whistle through one. We were glad to take shelter from it in a little hut the herd had built out of a one-time croft. It was a shadowed, mouldy place where the moor came in over the threshold. The door hung from its hinges and was too large for the hut, whose low roof had been made by stretching sticks across one another and covering them with a matting of bracken. Julia's head was on the dominie's shoulder, and the shadows of the sticks fell faintly across her face, making her look as though she were behind bars.

I was peeling the bark off a twig and thinking how sheltered and comfortable the draughty hut was compared to outside when the door suddenly jerked open. I thought it had been flung back by a sudden squall of wind, but my heart stood still as I looked over my shoulder and saw papa standing in the doorway.

His expression of amazement when he saw who was within chilled on his face as he gazed down at us, taking in every detail. I felt the paralysing sense of misgiving that I never outgrew and which always took hold of me when I saw his eyes narrow and his mouth compress. We rose to our feet, forgetting in our troubled haste that the roof was so low. He voiced no comment, for he was accompanied by Mr Ferguson, but he stood, upright and withdrawn, everything about him, from his thin nose to his alienating silence, making his displeasure felt more acutely than words.

Julia betrayed none of the disquietude she must have felt, only her face perhaps became a little flushed. But she introduced the dominie to Mr Ferguson with the same composure she would have shown had we met him in a drawing-room. The dominie, taken at a disadvantage, was ill at ease and became remote and silent as papa, while Julia conversed with Mr Ferguson with all her rallying, disarming charm.

"Pon my soul,'pon my soul,' he said with the diffuseness of a breathless man, 'we didn't think to find your sanctuary inhabited, did we, William? Don't let us chase you away, Miss Lockhart. We're on our way to see the Roman encampment, but I said to your father if he didn't find me a place where I could draw breath without being winded, I would expire.'

I do not think he had seen into the hut when Julia's head was on the dominie's shoulder, for he was a little behind papa, but the meeting in itself was untoward and he must have sensed tension from papa's protracted icy silence and the dominie's stiffness. An ardent fisherman, however, who pursued his hobby from morning to night in the face of his congregation's united disapproval, he was accustomed to shutting his eyes to the obvious. He now rose to the occasion with abandon, ostentatiously overlooking anything amiss to the extent of shaking hands warmly with Julia although he was seeing her again within the hour.

There was silence between us as we walked away until we were well out of earshot of the hut when Julia, waves of colour breaking over her face, turned to the dominie and said:

'Well, you were not very helpful, were you?'

'I am sorry,' he returned, 'but I could think of nothing to say.'

'It was not only that you stood and said nothing,' she retorted, swallowing, 'but, upon my word, you might have been in league with papa.'

'It was a very trying situation for your father,' he pointed out.

'Trying situation for papa!' she exclaimed angrily as a few flakes of snow began to fall uncertainly. 'Trying situation for papa! And do you think it was a pleasant and comfortable situation for me?—particularly when I knew that papa had wanted me expressly to help to entertain Mr Ferguson this afternoon, and I had made some trifling excuse because I wanted to be with you. Trying for papa! I assure you it is entirely your fault that a situation so trying for papa arose in the first place.' He attempted to speak but she would brook no interruption. 'It is because of you our meetings are secretive and stolen, is it not? I do not think you will deny that. Do you intend they should always be so? I, for one, despise and abominate concealment: there would be need of none of it once you came openly to the manse—'

'You know your father would never permit that,' he said. 'There is the difference in our religions for one thing.'

'And are we any nearer bridging that difficulty now than we were six months ago?' she demanded. 'Has a Catholic never married a Protestant before?'

There was a pause, a waiting pause which, for me, prolonged itself unbearably, although I do not think Julia noticed it, for she was arranging her own disordered thoughts. But as I walked beside the dominie through the snow that was now whirling thickly down, I found myself wondering if he had made himself believe that the difference in their religion stayed him from all possible action. Even then I realised that he confessed, never declared, his love, and was so afraid of happiness he had to do penance for any that came his way.

'I wonder if another thing has struck you,' Julia pursued hotly, 'and that is that papa will demand an explanation whenever Mr Ferguson leaves to-night.'

I felt her words pulled at him, that she was pinning him down, against his will, with her decision.

'I should have known,' he cried out, almost in agony, 'I should have known this would happen—it is all my fault.'

We clambered over the dyke on to the road where we stood, listening. The galloping of hooves came towards us and round the corner, with horses' heads bent against the blinding eddies of snow, posted a carriage. To our surprise it drew up a little past us, the door opened and a man jumped out. He came towards us, holding out both his hands to Julia, and I saw it was Edwin Strathern.

'Ah, Miss Lockhart,' he greeted her, 'this is well met. You must permit us to take you home dry-shod.'

'Indeed we should be obliged,' she assured him, with so sudden a brightness it might have been defiance. Particles of snow patterned her dark hair and her head was high in the air.

'I fear,' said Edwin Strathern, 'we have room only for two.' His glance, although it rested but a moment on the dominie, was so penetrating as to be almost a stare.

Handshakes followed and Mr Strathern excused again with regret to Mr MacDonald the incapacity of his carriage. There were confused good-byes and Julia and I climbed in beside Christine and her aunt. For a moment before we started forward, we saw, framed in the square of carriage window, the dominie standing at the roadside with white snow drifting soundlessly round him.

After Mr Ferguson left, Julia, strung-up and prepared with a more or less adequate answer for every challenge, waited for papa's certain displeasure to take the form of words. But the evening passed, and the following day came and went, without any enforced interview. He did not have her transcribe his letters as was his custom but sat alone, shut in his study, amongst his books with their old, rot-eaten calf batters and the snuffy smell peculiar to religious tomes. His continued silence played on Julia's nerves, and I would see her hands twisting together on her lap as she sat with her purposeful face shadowed in thought.

Emmy knew there was something troubling her sister and I think it was to keep Julia's thoughts from brooding that, on the Thursday, she suggested we should go a walk in the afternoon as well as our usual one in the morning. That she knew Julia was in love with the dominie, I never doubted, for Emmy was so quick in what Nannie called 'the uptak',' her perception was often put down to intuition. Perhaps she felt it that Julia did not confide in her, but Julia was well aware that Emmy had nothing in common with the dominie. She was apprehensive for both their sakes on the rare occasions they met, lest the dominie sensed he was being weighed in the balance and found wanting or lest Emmy was quickened into impatience.

Frost rimmed the grass in the garden and whitened all the trees when we set out in the afternoon. The snow had melted except in the blue shadows of the dykes and in the wood where it lay in patches sprinkled with pine-needles, like the footmarks of birds.

Because we had gone in the Auchendee direction in the morning, we turned our faces now towards Barnfingal. We walked as far as the gloomy spot in Mar woods where the gamekeeper hung on two boards the tails of weasels, stoats, badgers, and sometimes the bush of a fox or the corpse of a black hoody crow, as a warning to bird and beast what would befall them should they cross MacLeod's path.

The children were leaving the schoolhouse when we passed on our return. Some, before running home, were playing in the three-cornered, grass-grown plot of ground in front of the school. Their voices floated to us as they counted out who was to be It.

> *Onery, twaery, duckery, seven.*
> *Alama, crack, ten am eleven,*
> *Peem pom, it must be done,*
> *Come tettle, come total, come twenty-one.*

A sadness filled me as I watched, an aching sadness, not for things lost in this life, but in some other world. I suddenly felt wearied; it was all so old: the rough grass which generations of bare feet had never permitted to grow rank, the ploughed fields on either side, the one small stunted tree; and beyond, the tireless loch and lined mountains. The very rhyme they chanted was old as the groves of the Druids. Scattered on the grass, the jigging children gave me the uneasy impression of mites gambolling at the foot of an unseeing eternity.

We hastened our footsteps as we neared the manse, anxious to hurry home to firelit room and table spread for tea and Nannie telling us to take off our frosty shoes in the lobby.

I was shutting the gate behind us when we heard footsteps, and round the corner came some one's dwindled shadow, as though pointing out the way. It was followed by Simon Fraser, who was climbing slowly up the path, one arm behind his lean back, lifting his feet high as he always did as though he were ploughing through snow. He bade us 'Guid-evening' and passed on. One of the four elders, we knew he had been to see papa on church matters or something equally important, for he was clad in his Sabbath 'blacks'.

'Emmy,' Julia said, her voice full of dread as she turned to look after him, 'what do you think that man was seeing papa about?'

'The pews or the collection or perhaps some one's ill,' Emmy reassured her. 'Why, there are a dozen reasons.'

Julia made as though she had not heard and hurried down the path. Once inside the manse, Emmy ran upstairs but Julia went to papa's study.

'Papa,' she asked him, 'what was Simon Fraser come to see you about to-night?'

He was standing in the middle of the floor, his gaze bent in deep preoccupation on the faded carpet.

'It appears,' he answered, looking up and watching her coldly with keen eyes, 'that the dominie is a Roman Catholic and shall have to be asked to go.'

'They can't do that,' Julia said slowly, after a long pause, leaning against the table as though she had a pain in her side.

'Can't do what?' rapped out papa.

'They can't ask the dominie to go merely because his religion is different from ours.'

'But come, come, such a thing cannot be permitted in a Protestant community. The man is here on a mistaken footing.'

'That's untrue,' she cried out violently. Then, checking herself, said, 'It was their fault, not the dominie's, that they assumed he was a Protestant.'

'It does not signify whose fault it was; it is done now and shall have to be undone.'

'But why, papa?'

'No Roman Catholic would allow a Protestant to teach in their schools, and it is not fitting a Catholic should have the entire tuition of the loch children.'

'You know—you must know—any one would know that he could do children no harm, only good, the greatest good in the world. Papa, you will not stand by and let them do it. You have influence over these men, you can prevent it if you will, they will be guided by you. Why should he be sent away only because a disagreeable old man like Simon Fraser says so? You know you said yourself, papa, only the other day that you wondered when Simon Fraser would be done making most unwelcome discoveries. There was that other affair of—'

'This discovery is not wholly unwelcome.'

Julia advanced further into the room. She kept her eyes

on his face, trying to hide the apprehension that her voice revealed.

'Why, papa?' she questioned. 'What do you mean by that?'

'There need be no doubt of what I mean,' he replied, his gaze fixed on the top of her head. 'I wrote on Tuesday to the dominie to inform him that Lisbet's lessons would be discontinued.'

Julia drew back as though struck; still watching his face, her mouth moved, as if trying to piece together words that she could not utter.

'Why?' she faltered at last.

'Because,' his voice was deliberate, each word cold with meaning, 'I considered that even that association with the dominie of Barnfingal school was unprofitable to my family.'

'What right have you to say that?' The blood was draining back into Julia's face; and now when her words did come, they gathered in a torrent. 'What is there wrong about love? You loved mamma, didn't you? And married her because you loved her, and had children. What is the difference between you and her and a man who loves me and I who love him?'

'The difference of upbringing and surroundings to which you are each accustomed. We hear now his very religion is different from yours. A marriage between you and him would be disastrous and only lead to unhappiness.'

'How can you tell that?'

'I am many years older than you. An older person can see far ahead; a young person cannot see beyond the immediate present.'

'You say it will be disastrous if we marry,' she flamed at him. 'I say it will be disastrous if we don't. You live your own life, papa, and would permit no one else to live it for you. What right has any one, even you, to attempt to change and map out my life for me against my will? It is I who am living it, I who will make the disastrous marriage, I who will bear the consequences.'

'I refuse to allow you to take a step that I know you would regret, are bound to regret. A day will come, Julia, probably not far distant, when you will be grateful that you did not have your way.'

'I would not console yourself with that thought, papa.' Her tone had hardened and her face looked strained.

'There is no more to be said,' he replied, recoiling into his stiffness.

'No,' she agreed, 'too much has been said already,' and, turning, she left him alone in the room.

She trailed upstairs and I, not knowing what else to do, followed her. She sat down on the chair at the foot of her bed, without removing her outdoor clothes, and continued to stare into the middle of the room at nothing until, to distract her, I said her name. She turned her glance on me, moving her head.

'At least,' she said, giving voice to her thoughts, 'we know where we are now, exactly where we are.' She rose to her feet. 'Light the candle, will you, Lisbet?'

She took the articles and white-spotted muslin cloth from the dressing-table; then, bringing her blotter out of a drawer, began to write. Only once did she raise her head and that was to look round when she asked me if I would take a letter to him before supper that night. I sat on the edge of Emmy's bed and waited for it, looking up through the skylight at the darkening clouds, while she covered sheet after sheet with her large firm handwriting.

'Shall I wait for an answer?' I asked when she was ready and I was buttoning on my cape.

'There won't be time,' she replied, her face flushed with bending over her writing; 'there is so much for him to answer, but I have told him to send me a letter by one of the scholars as soon as he possibly can.'

I was not long in reaching Barnfingal and, as I crossed the playground, saw the dominie come out of the schoolroom, bending his head to avoid the low lintel of the roughly made door. Clothed in his own serenity, he was so tall and calm, one should have felt that here was a man on whose shoul-

ders one could rest the responsibility of the world. But as I
hurried forward to catch him before he entered his house,
I was aware of the same feeling of insecurity in him that I
had when I saw him after he had first kissed Julia. Now I
read a certain withdrawal in his startled surprise when he
saw who I was and I thrust her bulky letter into his hand.
Suddenly and quite incomprehensibly, I felt too young for
him—like a wind disturbing something that wished to
settle.

Although papa had not told me directly I was to have no more lessons from the dominie, I was well aware he knew that I knew his wishes on the matter. I felt guilty and apprehensive, therefore, as I hurried to the schoolhouse the next day; but Julia had pleaded with me to go. I think she expected he would make me the bearer of his answer to her letter.

'He'll have to tell me, Julia, what I know already,' I said to her, 'that papa doesn't want me to have any more lessons from him.'

'Yes, yes, I know,' she had replied.

'And I'll have to pretend to be surprised, Julia, and look as though I hadn't known.'

'Yes, yes, I know,' she had said again, and in the next breath prayed me to go.

The dominie was not in the schoolroom when I arrived, which perplexed me, for neither Julia nor I had thought of such an eventuality. I wondered if I were later than usual, for I had met no children on the brae, returning home from school, yet I knew I had set off at the customary time on the hall clock. I sat on a bench trying to puzzle out what I should do next while I totted up all ways the half-finished sum the dominie had chalked on the blackboard. Nothing is more depressing than an empty schoolroom. The one in which I sat wore a dingy, deserted look as though the children who had last conned lessons there had been of a generation ago and no one had entered it since.

When a quarter of an hour passed, I realised that the dominie was not returning to the schoolroom that afternoon and that, if I wanted to see him, I must go to his house.

75

My footsteps echoed hollowly as I walked down the room. Usually the schoolroom door was open and the door of the house shut, like a rebuff. To-day, however, I had had to push the schoolroom door a-jar and the door to the house was open wide to all comers. I hesitated for a moment, then put out my hand to knock on it when I gave a violent start.

'Whit we feel regret aboot, Mr MacDonald,' came the voice of Simon Fraser from within, so distinctly I might have been in the room with him, 'is that ye didna tak' us into your confidence to the extent o' telling us ye were a Roman Catholic.'

'It is not a question of excluding you from my confidence, Mr Fraser,' I heard the dominie reply, his voice shaking with perturbation, 'that I never knowingly did. I was not to know that what was natural as breathing to me would be unnatural to you. Never for a moment did I dream there would be antagonism because I was a Catholic.'

'It's a peety, Mr MacDonald, that ye hadna tauld us at the beginning and tested oor antagonism then.' I knew it was Naughton, the mole-catcher and elder, who spoke; he was an insignificant-looking man with a secretive smile always lurking on his lips.

'Mr Naughton,' it was the dominie speaking again, 'do you want me to understand that you think I purposely concealed telling you I was a Catholic?'

'Na, na, Mr MacDonald,' I heard Naughton hurriedly retract, and add lamely, 'but it is a peety, and a peety's a peety.'

'I cannot allow it to be said that I came here, determined to be dominie and so concealed the fact I was a Catholic. Not only from Mr Naughton, but from all here, I have the impression that is what is thought.' There followed a silence in which the very house seemed to join. 'I have a right to say there was nothing to hide and I hid nothing. After all, you only conceal what you are ashamed of, do you not? You are all proud of your religion; I, too, am proud of mine.'

'If that's the case, Mr MacDonald, the sooner ye gang the better and the sorrier we are ye came.' When I heard the tones of Gow, the farmer, I realised each of the four elders would be within: Simon Fraser and Naughton, Gow, who despite his fair spade beard had the face of a beautiful woman, and MacLeod, the gamekeeper, a swarthy, hirsute man.

'Mebbe it is as weel,' MacLeod now said reflectively; 'ye sit up unco late at nicht.'

'And what has that to do with it?' came the dominie's astonished voice.

'Aweel, it doesna gie a place a guid name,' Simon Fraser put in.

'Only on Wednesday,' Gow informed them, 'MacLean from Maragdow, on the ither side o' the loch, said to me at the market, passing-like, "Your dominie canna be o'er wide-awake for his scholars of a morning."'

'Onywey, if ye hadna been going,' came Fraser's voice again, 'we had meant to say to ye that we thocht ye were wasting o'er muckle o' your ain and the bairns' time telling them so muckle aboot floors.'

'They can see floors ony day,' said some one else.

'And ye havena gi'en the tawse ainse syne ye've been here.'

'It's no natural-like for bairns na to need the tawse.'

'I mind saying at the verra beginning afore Mr MacDonald came,' MacLeod remarked, 'that we werena gi'en near lang enow to think it a' o'er. We only had twa days to mak' oor decision, ye mind, no counting the Sabbath.'

'It was ye, Naughton, wha wanted things settled in a hurry. Ye mind, when I bespoke for ma cousin, ye said it would be o'er lang for us to wait until he could come frae Aberdeen to see us.'

'I thocht it a peety, Fraser, the bairns should lose ony mair days' schooling.'

'Weel, it's been a peety, Naughton, a grave peety, for noo they'll lose mair in the end. It's a guid thing for us ma cousin has na been fixed by one ither body.'

'Aweel, Fraser, stikkit meenisters aften have deeficulty in finding poseetions for themsel's.'

'It's no a case o' deeficulty, Naughton; it's a case o' Providence working for us.'

'We had better be for telling Mr MacDonald when we want him to gang,' pointed out Gow.

'We canna gie ye langer than Monday, Mr MacDonald,' declared Simon Fraser, 'for I have written telling ma cousin to come wi' a' his gear on the Tuesday coach.'

'I understand.'

'Then we will bid ye guid-day.'

I heard their heavy tramp across the floor. There was nowhere I could hide outside, nor had I time to run away or the presence of mind to pretend I was only arriving. Panic seized me. Before I realised what I was doing, I found myself pressed between the wall and the open door.

I saw them, through a crack in the door, file past, so near to me and real that I felt faintly sick. MacLeod's broad back, clothed in hairy raploch, brought up the rear.

'We micht have kent,' I heard him say, 'no to have ta'en a MacDonald.'

The house was very still after they left, so still that the rasp
the door made as I drew myself from behind it sounded like
a screech. I waited, my heart beating unevenly, for the noise
to summon the dominie into the passage, but he did not
stir. For one moment before I turned and fled, I saw into
the room in which he stood, his back towards me. It was a
bare room, as though he had not yet unpacked, and was filled
with the loud ticking of a wag-at-the-wa' clock which, as its
pendulum jerked its shadow across the wall, seemed to be
making up frenziedly for lost time.

I ran from the schoolhouse, my footsteps hurrying after
me. As I mounted the brae, I saw Emmy and Julia, Emmy's
full skirt swinging like a bell, disappear into Mrs Wands'
cottage. They had not noticed me, and when I came to the
cottage door I tapped softly.

Mrs Wands' kitchen was dark when I entered, as though
it were dusk outside, for the rafters were low, the window
was tiny and the sun had moved round to the gable-end of
the cottage. Shadows tottered on the walls, great misshapen
shadows of the hams hanging from the rafters, the hook of
the swee and the back of a chair, like instruments of torture.
They shifted over the old woman in the bed, who stirred as
I entered, moving her head on the bolster to see who I was.

'So it's ye, come ben, come ben,' she welcomed me. 'I was
juist saying to your sisters that it's a lang day syne I've seen
ony o' ye. Ay, it's been a lang winter. The lambs arena guid
this year for the winter's been so hard the sheep are lean. Eh,
Miss Julia, ye'll ne'er guess wha sat on yon chair afore ye.'

We thought of all manner of people to please her, from
Dr Malcolm to the Marquis's grieve, but at each wrong

guess she cried out with gratification, 'Na, na, na him,' until Emmy suddenly clapped her hands and guessed the Marquis himself.

'Na him, but his wife,' she said with high delight, and went on, lowering her voice as though her Grace might hear, 'and the Lord hasna made her better looking than ony ither body although He has made her a Marchioness.'

'And what did she say to you?' Emmy asked excitedly.

'She sat on yon chair, juist as Miss Julia's doing noo, and speired frae me this and that and hoo lang I had been leeing here, and shook her heid when I tauld her and said, "Ah me" aince or twice. So I juist said to her I could see and hear as mony a one half ma age couldna. And then she said, "Mistress Wands, I believe ye have a verra nice piece o' china and I wunnered if ye would gie it to me and I would mak' it weel up to ye."'

'What piece of china did she mean, Mrs Wands?'

'It was the auld blue dish o' ma graundmither's she meant—I mind Mr Urquhart when he cam' ben last summer turning it upside doon to read something on its foot. I said I was sorry she couldna have it as I kept ma butter in it, and she said she would bring me anither dish, a better dish for ma butter wi' na so mony corners to it. But I tauld her ma butter wouldna taste the same somewey oot o' ony ither dish than ma grannie's. She left soon aifter that,' she finished reminiscently.

'I'm glad she came and not the Marquis,' Emmy said discursively. 'They say she's nicer than he is. He used to ogle mamma most disgracefully in Princes Street in Edinburgh.'

'I've only seen him aince, when he gave the baptism stane to the kirk, and I thocht to masel' no a' the baptism stanes in Christendom will keep ye oot o' hell. But he comes o' a guid family, e'en supposing they did get a' their land by murdering ither folk. But they're in a sad way these days whit wi' thirlages and debts. When ma graundfaether was alive, they had four castles in a', and noo they have but twa. Ay, ay, there's na muckle laund to earl it o'er noo. But whit wi' her veesit and a' this strumash o'er the dominie, I havena kent which side to lee on.'

'What have you heard about the dominie?' inquired Julia, her passivity suddenly wakening into interest.

'I've been hearing things aboot him, on and aff, a' winter,' she answered. 'I mind saying to ye when ye were here afore that he was unbekent, na like ither folk, and that's whit ither folk began to feel aboot him.'

'How do you mean "not like other people"?' Emmy asked curiously.

'Weel, Miss Emmy, he did things ither folk wouldna or couldna do. I'll tell ye a thing he did that I saw wi' ma ain een. It was one day when Dookit was awa'—the day ye gave your picnic, Miss Julia, wi' your freends frae Dormay. Ian MacPhee had caught some trout in the burn and on his way hame he cam' ben and left me wi' twa. The dominie cam' o'er to see me a meenit aifter Ian and said he would cook the fish for me. I saw him gut them in the twinkling o' an e'e. They were lifeless as stanes when he put them in the pan but na sooner had he turned his back and afore they began e'en to sizzle, they lepit in the air like live things and fell on to the floor. I tell ye, I wouldna have eaten yon trout if it was to cost me ma life.'

'But, surely, Mrs Wands,' Julia protested impatiently, 'you don't think the dominie made the trout jump out of the pan when he was not even touching it?'

'I've seen trout cooked a' the days o' ma life, Miss Julia, and I've ne'er seen them behave like yon trout. They say he casts spells o'er folk as well as o'er things—o'er the bairns to keep them quiet and o'er ithers wha arena ignorant like bairns.' Her eyes sought ours and dwelt on Julia.

'That is nonsense,' Emmy said briskly; 'people don't cast spells nowadays.'

'If they could cast them in the past, Miss Emmy, whit's to hinder them doing it still? I think he cast one o'er me, for when folk cam' ben here during the winter, telling me this and that aboot him, many's the time I oped ma mouth to say he was a Roman Catholic and I ne'er yet foond the words.'

'But the dominie was always so quiet,' persisted Emmy, 'the last person, I would have imagined, to be whispered about and have stories hung round him.'

'When folk are as quiet as him, Miss Emmy, there's something hid in them. They say his licht was always the last to gang oot in Barnfingal and some nichts he went oot and walked by himsel' amang the hills and didna come hame till the early oors o' the morning.'

'But really, Mrs Wands, there is nothing evil about that. Why shouldn't he, if he wanted to? He was busy all day.'

'It's no natural, Miss Julia, it's no natural at a' to gang walking when ither men sleep. Whit was he doing a' by himsel' on the hills wi' na one to see him? Like as not waiting to midnicht to ca' up the deil frae a stane to speak wi' him.'

'It is wrong of people to speak like that,' Julia said tempestuously, 'wrong and wicked to see evil where there is none. There is nothing unnatural in the dominie's walking at night, alone with his thoughts, when he felt he had the world to himself. He interfered with no one, and did no one any harm. Why then should people try to harm him with hard thoughts?'

'Aweel, Miss Julia, mony's the hard thing I've heard said against him ben this kitchen, richtly or wrang. They a' kent there was something na richt aboot him e'en afore they kent he was a Roman Catholic. I mind John Ferguson, and he's no a back-biting man, telling me he aince thocht to himsel' that he would ask the dominie to gie his Rob some extra schooling that he micht win a bursary mebbe, syne there wasna enow work for him on the croft. He didna tell ony one, e'en his wife, whit he was thinking but set aff for the schoolhouse and saw the dominie some distance aff, coming towards him alang the road frae the direction o' the manse. When they cam' up to one anither, afore John Ferguson e'en oped his mouth, the dominie said to him, "Ay, maist certainly, Mr Ferguson, I'll teach your Rob if he waits aifter school oors, and I dinna see why he shouldna win a bursary to himsel'. It will be a graund help to ye for ye have your ither lads to help ye wi' your laund." Na, na. They micht have kent a' alang frae his een mischief lay in him, for he wasna marked wi' twa deeferent een for ony guid.'

'I rather like his two different eyes,' Emmy said thoughtfully, 'they make you wonder what he really is seeing. How did they find out he was a Catholic, Mrs Wands?'

The old woman straightened herself as well as she could in the box-bed and set swinging the frayed rope that dangled above her.

'When Homish MacLeod fell frae the Dingwall's loft,' she said. 'If there's ony fashery in this clachan, there's a MacLeod in it somewhere. His leg bent under him and he fell on top o' it. The dominie cam' running to him, and pu'd at his leg and crackit it and held it in his twa haunds. Mebbe he thocht Homish had swooned but Homish had done na such thing, and he heard him saying, saft-like to himsel':

*The Lord rade, and the foal slade;*
*He lighted, and he righted.*
*Set joint to joint, bone to bone,*
*And sinew to sinew,*
*Heal, in the Holy Ghost's name.*

Her voice had sunk to a whisper. 'Homish was running aboot next day wi' no e'en a hirple. He tauld his faether whit the dominie had done to him and said as he was doing it, and his faether tauld Simon Fraser wha didna like the soond o' it at a'. He said he had been thinking for a lang time back, Miss Julia, that it was an unbecoming thing for the dominie to walk seeven miles every Sabbath to attend Mr Urquhart's kirk when he could hear a better sermon by far frae your faether only two miles awa'.' She pulled up the counterpane into a poke with her fingers and then flattened it with her hand. 'Yon was the day MacLauchlan o' Dormay was passing through Barnfingal wi' his shepherd, and Simon Fraser met him on the road and asked if he had e'er seen the dominie in Mr Urquhart's kirk. "I've ne'er clapped een on him," said MacLauchlan, "and if he went to the kirk, I couldna miss seeing him." So Simon Fraser went to the schoolhouse and chappit on the door, e'en though the bairns were at their lesson. And when the dominie cam', he said, "Whit meenister do ye sit onder, Mr MacDonald?" And he answered, "Na meenister, Mr Fraser, but the priest in the chapel at Inverlui." When Simon Fraser heard that, he turned and left him and changed into his blacks and went straight to see your faether, Miss Julia.'

The next day was perhaps the longest I have ever endured, waiting for word that never came, listening, while we were at meals, for footsteps to sound on the garden path, looking up each time Nannie entered the room to see if she held a letter in her hand.

It struck me then for the first time how oblivious we are of those with whom we live. Emmy might have sensed Julia's underlying unrest, but mamma, talking at length of the letter she had received that morning from Mr Scrivener, the lawyer, and of Nannie's earache, was quite unaware there was anything the matter with her eldest daughter. As for papa, since the evening Julia had faced him in his study, he had been like a closed book, and sometimes left the table without having made one remark during the whole of a meal.

I was asleep by the time Julia came to bed and had only a vague recollection of seeing her, through half-opened, misted eyes, in her long white nightgown, blowing out the candle, but in the early hours of the morning I was awakened by hearing her speak. It was a few seconds before I realised she had been talking in her sleep, murmuring endearingly words that sounded like 'Dear darling.' I knew when people talked in their sleep it betokened bad dreams from which one should awaken them, but she had spoken so gently that I was wondering if I should disturb her, when suddenly she sat up in bed and called out sharply, 'Who's there?'

'There's no one there—no one, Julia,' I assured her; 'you've only been dreaming.'

I could see her faintly through the greying dark, with her

black hair ruffled and her face turned towards the door. Emmy stirred beside me.

'What is it?' she asked sleepily.

'It wasn't like dreaming,' Julia said, and I knew she shivered—Nannie would have said some one was walking over her grave. 'I felt—some one bending over me, I could swear some one bent over me—trying to say something, make me understand.'

'There's no one in the room but us,' said Emmy, now thoroughly wide awake. 'It's been a bad dream, Julia. I'll come and sleep with you, if you like.'

I could not fall asleep properly after that and only dozed fitfully, hearing through uneasy dreams the window chattering in its frame and feeling glad when it was time to rise.

That Sunday was always known on the loch as 'Mr Lockhart's Blaw Sabbath' for the wind, or blow, was so loud he could scarcely make himself heard. I sat between mamma, who was always so pleasantly interested in whom was at church, and Julia, who kept running her gloved finger along the grain in the wood of the pew. The critical congregation sat forward in the deep pews, their faces all gazing pulpit-wards as they turned over in their deliberative minds each head of the minister's sermon.

At the evening service papa had to tell his dispersed congregation to come nearer to him because of the noise of the wind. We all sat crowded together in the four front pews, thinking each furious blast that set the church rocking must surely be the last, until another yet more violent would come, drowning papa's stern raised voice, which sounded over-loudly through the creaking church when the wind died into the distance to marshal its forces for the next assault.

I went early to our bedroom to undress that night and was plaiting my hair when Julia entered the room. Her face was dead white and there were wet purple shadows below her darkened eyes. The door slammed behind her and she stood with her back to it.

'Lisbet,' she said, 'he would never go—would he?

—without seeing me? Tell me he wouldn't—for God's sake, tell me he wouldn't.'

'Of course he wouldn't, Julia, of course he wouldn't. What made you think such a thing?'

'Nannie said just now, when I was in the kitchen, that Alec Gow told her when he came with the milk this evening that the dominie had left last night. But it's not true, it can't be true. Why should he go without seeing me after all that has happened between us? And I dare not question Nannie too closely. I must know to-night, or I will go mad.'

'I'll go, Julia, and find out.'

'Yes, Lisbet, you go. Go now, and oh, go quick.'

Boughs of trees swooped as though to catch me as I hurried up the path. I tried to escape from the wind but it wrestled with me all the way to Barnfingal. Everything was blackened out with storm and I had difficulty finding the dominie's house, for it was unlit. I reached it at last and knocked on the door, shaking it by the handle when no one came. It was not locked and I went inside. I called the dominie by name at the foot of the steep stairs and then felt terrified at the sound of my voice in the empty house.

There was no movement as in the manse, for there were no trees to throw shadows. I looked into the room where I had seen the dominie standing on Friday, and stared within until my eyes grew accustomed to the darkness. Then it had looked as though he had not yet unpacked; now, knowing he was supposed to be gone, it looked as though he had not yet packed, for it was the same as it had been on Friday, exactly the same, with his jacket hanging on the corner of the door, his books on the mantelshelf and a pair of brogues on the floor. Only the clock was silent: its white face gazed down at me from the wall, as if startled, with its transfixed hands pointing to twenty-past three.

I ran from the schoolhouse as though pursued. He could not be gone, of course he could not be gone with the door of his house unlocked and all his belongings still in the rooms. But I must find out from some one for sure, before I returned to Julia, to put her heart at rest.

The MacPhees' light blinked through their window deepset in the whitewashed wall. As I reached it, young Ian loomed out of the byre. I could not make him hear me above the wind and he took me into the kitchen where men's wet clothes were strung on a line stretched from wall to wall. They filled the room with a steamy close smell and a vapour which was pricked with, what seemed to me, rows of countless eyes, for heads turned inquiringly as I entered and bodies rose from seats.

'Why, missy—'

'I have a message for Mr MacDonald, the dominie,' I began.

Eyes swam round to me from all different corners of the kitchen.

'Mr MacDonald is awa',' said MacPhee.

'You are quite sure?' I managed to ask.

'The coo's had the milk-pox,' Morag explained helpfully, 'and Ian was sitting up wi' her a' last nicht. He heard him pass alang the road aifter midnicht.'

'Weel aifter midnicht,' amplified Ian. 'Aboot three it would be, and I ne'er heard him come back.'

'He's walkit oot withoot e'en taking his money,' said MacPhee, waving his pipe in the air to emphasise his words. 'They're leaving everything juist as he left it and the door unlockit until the morn's morn in case he comes back, for it's his hoose until then. But he'll na come back.'

'Na,' said Ian, 'he didna soond to me as though he would come back.'

I left them and heard the door shut as I began to climb the brae. Half-way home I had to stop through sheer inability to hasten any more. From a far distance, through the loneliness in a lull of wind, I heard a grouse on the moor scream, 'Go back! Go back!' I stood quite still and, summoning up every nerve in my body, willed with all my strength that the dominie would come back.

When I reached the manse gate I knew, with that fatality one usually only has in dreams, that he would never return.

*Book Three*

Snow fell, obliterating the sheep tracks, blocking the peat roads, ridging the screes. Beyond the manse, shuttered in with trees, the wind paced. Ice traced fern patterns on the window panes and chuckled in the rapids of the burn. It grew so wild and stormy the postman came on a horse with the mails and we could no longer hear the ticking of the clock when we gathered round the table for meals, our faces lamp and fire burnished. In the parlour Emmy sat at the piano, her fingers racing up and down her scales with a light, bright finality, until I felt all life was bound by those undeviating notes.

On twelfth night Nannie told us daylight increased by the length of a deer's leap, and Candlemas Day was rainy, which meant the worst of winter was past. With the cuckoo came the Gowk Storm and August brought the Lammas floods.

Life swung by to walks on the moor and sewing and reading and wondering what next day would bring. The scent of briar roses gave place to the honey-sweet smell of vivid bell heather growing in tussocks on the shelves of rocks, and we began to look for blaeberries on our walks. The tiny fir tree in the garden now tipped the top of the dyke. Sunday broke up each week for us, and regular as the event of Tuesday itself Mr Urquhart came to visit papa. They were now at that trying, easily offended stage of intimacy when they had heard everything each had to say, but, through long custom, neither could keep away from the other.

On Hallowe'en the three of us sat with Nannie in the kitchen. Outside, spirits, released for one night in the year, rode on the wind, rending the trees in their fury.

The window darkened as their shadow spasms crossed it and we could hear them cracking and groaning.

I had always loved to sit in the kitchen beside Nannie with Julia and Emmy. No matter how the wind thundered and raged outside, I had always felt quite safe there. But now something had destroyed this sense of security, though all was the same as it once was from fitful flame to singing kettle. I no longer exulted with the storm in the glory of its strength; it sounded piteous to me now, the shut-out, unhappy wind. Unlikely things happened in this world—might take place perhaps before the kettle came to the boil, and the storm gusts rattling at the door were like some one trying to get in.

Emmy sat with her hat perched on top of her knee. Rain had soaked it that afternoon and she was working the wet brim into a different shape with her fingers, to add some variety to the wearing of it.

'Let it be noo,' advised Nannie, 'or ye'll have it so shapeless it will be flapping all roond your face and ye'll be saying the morn's morn ye canna wear it. Let time work for ye.'

'Do you believe, Nannie,' Emmy asked confidingly, looking down at her stained fingers, 'in leaving everything with God, or do you think we should make efforts to change things?'

'Is it to God you leave it?' Julia said suddenly, with a bitterness beyond her years. 'I sometimes think everything we do is prompted by some part of us wanting it, even unknown to ourselves. When things happen—'

'Things dinna juist happen, Miss Julia,' Nannie put in quickly, 'there is a reason for a' things.'

'But the world is so full of man now,' Emmy agreed with Julia, 'that their wills and actions are bound to influence what happens. It would have been easier at the beginning of time, when the world was young and fierce and untried; then there was no sorrow banking up, not so many things crowding out God and obscuring His will.'

'God's will is as clear noo as it was then,' Nannie said finally, 'but mebbe we are no so clear aboot looking for it whit wi' always wanting whit we havena been gi'en. Ye can do withoot so muckle ye ne'er thocht ye could—ye can do withoot almost anything. Things are no harder than they were and naething mak's a man so weak as o'er-peetying o' himsel'.' She poured mamma's hot milk into the waiting tumbler, placed it on a saucer and, with it shaking like a flame in her hand, left the kitchen.

We turned our heads as some autumn leaves, blown by a capful of wind, pattered against the window.

'That means winter is coming,' Julia said in a flat voice beside us. 'Another winter just like last—I don't think I could bear it.'

I do not know whether she ever expected the dominie would write or, if she did, when she gave up hope. Perhaps when she heard and made herself believe that he was the man to enter the monastery at Fort Halliam, over a year ago, towards the end of April.

That the dominie could be allowed to disappear from Barnfingal into nowhere was incompatible with the temperament of the crofters and shepherds, for now he was as absorbing a topic of conversation as long-dead Florah of the Evil Eye or the vanished Lady of Fingal. Each small piece of news about him was eagerly repeated and nursed until a fairly consecutive hearsay account was linked together of his journey to Fort Halliam.

Enoch MacDiarmid heard at Mhoreneck that a tall man, a total stranger, had been seen to pass through the village about eight on the very morning the dominie had so early left Barnfingal. He was noticed at Polman's Tryst drinking from a burn. The fleeing-tailor, arriving on his yearly round, took the pins out of his mouth to tell of meeting him on the road through the Pass of Naver; he minded the meeting well, for he stopped to ask him the way to Fort Halliam.

Heads were nodded gravely at the mention of that name, for every one knew that only fishermen lived there, fishermen and silent monks withdrawn into their grey mausoleum of a monastery.

The last we ever heard of him was some years later when Alec Gow returned from Fort Halliam, where he had been seeing about a certain breed of sheep, and related there was a brother in the monastery who was known amongst the villagers as 'the monk wi' the twa een'.

Youth would pass humbly there and visions tremble in the prayer-bound air. Did the days go swiftly by, or did the passage of a bird's shadow take long to flit across his book? Could his spirit go at will through the byres and dairies and dusty barns of his childhood home; did it ever visit the Barnfingal schoolroom and the familiar howffs where he used to meet Julia and me, or did it spend itself shunning even the memory of them, trying to believe they had never been? Did he still find himself caught in other men's minds, groping amongst their thoughts as he heard the brothers round him singing as one? Did he ebb and flow, a lifeless thing, on the tide of each new day, or, fortified by prayer, did he keep himself so tuned and strung that Christ could play?

He was dead to us after that spring, and Julia's mind had gone like ice. We who lived with her could make no impression upon it. Our comfort, our moods, our thoughts, did not touch her; she was locked within her numbed self beyond our reach.

The dreariness of her voice when she made the remark about winter appalled me. I had been so ready to believe that at last the past was being forgotten and now, for one bared second, I glimpsed the gaping emptiness of her outlook.

Emmy and she came late to bed that night and I heard them whispering to one another long after twelve o'clock. The following day they went for a walk together from which Julia returned brighter than she had been for months. She spent all that afternoon writing by herself upstairs and in the evening she sat with Emmy in the bedroom, from where I could hear in the parlour the rise and fall of their murmuring voices.

Several days later I went to Gow's Farm for some extra milk for Nannie. Mrs Gow kept me, I remember, while she picked hairy gooseberries and red and black currants from the laden bushes in her garden for me to take home, and gave me tea in her parlour which was filled with the sleepy smell of geraniums.

I started for home about five o'clock, swinging the basket of fruit on my arm and singing below my breath. It had been raining, a soft bright rain, and I noticed on the muddy road at the manse gate tracks of carriage wheels that had not, I felt sure, been there when I set out.

The house seemed curiously silent when I entered, as though something had happened and it was experiencing an aftermath of quiet. I went into the parlour to give mamma Mrs Gow's remembrances, and saw her sitting, her hands idle on her sewing, at the fire.

'Oh, Lisbet,' she exclaimed, looking up at me with blinking eyes, 'you'll never guess who has called.' Mamma often annoyed papa by asking him to guess things, but this afternoon she waited for no conjectures. 'Edwin Strathern,' she pursued breathlessly. 'He has asked Julia to marry him and now they are engaged.'

The notes of a bird in the garden outside sounded so piercingly clear it might have been in the room, and I heard distinctly the trailing of an insect's wings on the window-pane.

'He was so excited,' mamma's voice was continuing, 'and could hardly take his eyes from her—as though, if he did, she would disappear! It is really a very suitable marriage, although he is so elderly, for Julia after all has always been rather old for her years. It is not as though it were Emmy.'

Edwin Strathern heaped gifts on us all—'He is so *beautifully* kind,' mamma would say. Scarcely a mail passed without something from him coming to the manse, a book for me, a fan for Emmy, gloves for Julia or a shawl for mamma. Under cover of Christmas they arrived in a positive spate; even Nannie was not forgotten when the many different shaped boxes came to be opened. Never once did he arrive at the manse with empty hands and when Julia protested, he would assure her he had quite forgotten to bring anything for her. Sometimes he and Emmy kept up the play that he really had forgotten until after he left, when Julia would find her packet hidden under the tea-cosy at supper or hear a rustle of paper when she threw back the bedclothes at night.

He agreed admirably with mamma and their mutual good spirits kindled each other into excitability. Sometimes when we were all laughing, I would realise that in the general merriment Julia seemed oddly out of tune. Yet he was so fond of her and watched her with so kindly an expression in his deep-set eyes that sometimes she made one impatient.

I think he would have given her anything she cared to ask and this attitude seemed almost to irritate Julia. It was as though she resented that he made things so easy for her, and often with him she was as difficult as she could be, fastening on details to expand into differences. Once she quarrelled with him most provocatively when, in answer to her question whether, if they were all drowning, he would save his mother or her first, he reluctantly replied his duty would be towards his mother. She confided the matter to Emmy, who set her laughing in spite of herself by asking briskly, 'Can Edwin swim?'

96

Once or twice she tried him too far and they had violent quarrels, when he left the manse in a rage. Julia would become conscience-stricken then, and ask us if we thought he were quite safe and if we were sure nothing was happening to him on the journey home, and had Emmy no premonitions about him. She would take out her blotter and I would see her writing him long involved letters in which she put herself so forcibly in the right that one found oneself wondering how one had ever doubted whether she were—letters with perhaps one loving message that brought him posting to the manse in all his ardour.

Christine's Aunt Bertha was the only unlively person during that festive season and she was wrapped in unrelieved gloom, for her brother had at last done what for sixteen years she had dreaded he would do. She was a woman always full of regrets who would join in nothing and then complain bitterly that she was left out of everything. It was tacitly agreed between her and Julia that they would not share the same home—no, she would set up house for herself, although she was growing an old woman.

The prospect of a young step-mother raised no resentment in Edwin Strathern's children. For one thing, neither of his sons remained at home for any length of time. They were an unintimate family, not bound to each other inevitably as are those who share the same experiences, but each going his own way and knowing little of the others. As for Christine, it was only a matter of months until she would marry Stephen Wingate and sail with him to India to join his regiment.

A few weeks before her marriage, Julia went with Emmy and me to St. Andrews for some ten days. It was the first time I had ever left the manse and I must have looked on everything with the eyes of an absorbed foreigner; yet I felt remotely familiar with this town of narrow wynds and shadowed pends as one feels familiar with anything, however strange, that answers one as beautiful. I burst into tears, I remember, when I caught my first sight of the sea. That was the last time the three of us were ever to be together for any period longer than an afternoon, and in memory

those days have become imbued for me with a rarity, never
to be recaptured, that sets them apart from all others.

It was March and the elds of weeping willow trees were
leafless. We walked into the flat country, among the red
fields of Fife, where little red-tiled cottages were hidden in
clumps of trees. We poked among the rocks in land-locked
pools made iridescent by sea-weed, and marvelled over the
simplest limpet. But best of all we loved to walk along
the stretch of gleaming-wet sands, looking for tiny joined
shells like angels' prayer-books to give to Emmy, watching
wan ships in the far distance, or stopping to ponder over
blind-looking jelly-fish thrown up by the swelling tide.
When I saw the sweep of sky joining the sea at the pale
horizon, I thought of the light, waning to wax, imprisoned
in the globe of the world. And as my thoughts ebbed and
flowed to the drow of the sea, I thought of the earth after
millions of years when life has left it, like a shell worn with
holes, filled only with windy vibrations: the faint echo of
the sea, the whisper of spent rain, a weak sighing as of
prayer.

Julia liked the town best where we looked from grey
streets through old houses into sunlit back gardens whose
trees had been planted centuries ago. I loved to wander
amongst the ruins of castle and cathedral standing entombed
in their own silence, but Emmy liked best the swept freedom
of the shore where sea-gulls hurried on pink legs before the
tide. I see her again holding her skirts above her pretty
knees as she paddled at the waves' edge and laughed over
her shoulder to Julia when she told her she would catch
her death of cold.

We had rooms in a house on the shady side of South
Street kept by a Mrs Lonie, who told us endless stories in
a sing-song voice after she brought in our meals, standing
at the door with her elbows in her hands. Sometimes she
read our fortunes from the teacups, promising us Closed
Bargains, Tall Men, Anchors, Word from Across Water,
and Rings by the score.

'I wish,' Emmy said when we were at tea on our last

day, 'Mrs Lonie could tell us who our Tall Men are,' and she picked out a leaf floating on top of her tea and placed it on the back of her hand. 'Whom do you think this Stranger is coming to visit us? He is not too tall and not too small but just a nice in-between. I'll tell you when to expect him—he'll need to be quick if he wants to find us here. Why,' she exclaimed, 'he's coming to-day—just when I have packed my blue frock.'

As we were finishing tea, we heard a horse's hooves coming down the street and some moments later a reverberating knock sounded on Mrs Lonie's door. She entered our room in a flurry to tell us that a gentlemen, whose name she had not quite caught, had called to see us, and Stephen Wingate appeared from behind her.

His home was quite near St. Andrews, he informed Julia, and it did not seem right somehow to let us go without seeing us, so he had ridden over to ask if we would call next day on his mother. Julia told him we were leaving on the morrow, and when he said how sorry he was—he spoke with a slight but not unattractive stutter—he looked from Julia to me and from me to Julia, his blue eyes studiously avoiding Emmy as though he did not care to see her.

'I did not know you lived near St. Andrews,' Julia remarked.

He seemed a little at unease but replied that, yes, he did.

'I could have been almost positive,' continued Julia, puzzled, 'that Christine told me your home was at Fortgall.'

I saw him redden. 'That is where I do live,' he admitted.

'Good heavens,' Julia exclaimed, 'it must have taken you hours to come.'

'It's within comfortable riding distance,' he assured her defensively.

'It all depends, of course, what you call "comfortable riding distance,"' she retorted, stiffening, and I saw that for some reason she was not pleased.

She grew warmer later when we went on the shore for our last walk. White clouds, like spreading wings, stretched across the bright sky when we set out, but we walked so far that when we turned to go back, dusk had deepened in the town and the grey rocks on the shore were like old men looking out to sea.

I always had little to say to strangers and had not yet learnt to say that little; but Stephen Wingate kept up a flowing conversation with Julia in which Emmy did not join. She walked apart from us, her hair blowing back over her fur cap.

'Come nearer to us, Emmy!' Julia called. 'It's most uncompanionable walking at that distance.'

'I always feel about your sister Emmy,' Stephen said with sudden malice, 'that she never finds her company worth saying anything to.'

Emmy turned her head to look at him calmly. I saw his gaze falter as it met hers.

'It was nice seeing him,' Julia remarked after he was gone, 'but I wish he hadn't come, somehow—the Stratherns may think it strange his visiting us at all that distance.'

'Why shouldn't he come if he wanted to?' demanded Emmy. 'And what does it matter if they do think it strange? They're not his keepers.'

A faint grey mist blew before the wind when we drove home from Dormay. I saw phantoms shape in it and white horses form as it came down the road towards us; while the wind cut chasms through it, pulled it into wisps and disbanded it in shreds like smoke.

A bird chattered and flew low across our path as we walked down the winding brae to the manse. I had never before noticed how the trees, bent one way by the wind, pressed back on the house, nor been conscious until then of the curious smell of damp, like old sweet apples, that clung to the creaking stairway.

We arrived home to find that papa had caught a chill which mamma and he were afraid was developing into something serious. Dr Malcolm came that afternoon to see him, entering in his boisterous way as though there were more than one of him. Papa, who always feared the worst when he himself fell ill and expected the best when it was any one else, was not consoled to be told,

'Only bronchitis, William, that's all. Nothing at all to make you look as though your last day had come—why, you're good for years yet. Our destinies lie not in our stars but in our bodies. You'll have to stay a-bed for a while, of course, but you won't be averse to that with all those varying aches and pains—it's a wise doctor who knows what his patient wants. You had better write to the Presbytery, Mrs Lockhart, to send another man, as it may be some weeks before your husband is up and about. I'll call over again to-morrow. It's a thankless task being a doctor in this district, I assure you, with the miller's mother telling me this morning she doesn't hold with doctors as all they can do is turn your stomach into an apothecary's shop! "If ma Maker wants me," I was informed, "no all the doctors in Christendom can keep me in this world." I tell you, I felt as though I were competing with the Almighty for her. Yes, a thankless job I'd change with no other. If the patient pulls through, it is because of his splendid constitution; if he doesn't, it's the fault of the doctor. I'll send some medicine over for your husband by the ferryman so that he can have it to-night.'

Mamma wrote that evening to the Presbytery and the minister to relieve papa arrived at the manse on Saturday in time to take the services on the morrow. Mamma described him to papa as seemingly a painstaking, conscientious young man, but somehow I had not thought of him as youthful. The only other locum tenens papa had ever had was a Mr Stevenson who came, years ago, when papa caught whooping-cough from Emmy; he had been a diffident young man, so afraid of overstaying his welcome that he had not attempted any visiting. But no such scruples beset Mr Boyd, who went where he listeth although he might be as unwelcome as a red-haired first-foot.

His face wore an habitual outraged expression, and the top part of his figure was shaped at the back like a kite, while he walked with a gait that invited mimicry. I suppose it was wrong of us to make sport of him, but his very attributes, admirable in any one else, were so exaggerated by pretentiousness and solemnity that one felt almost bound to ridicule him.

Emmy said whenever she saw him that we must know what to expect. He came downstairs that evening with a large flat portfolio of flower paintings under his arm. We would have enjoyed it if we had each been allowed to glance through it, but Mr Boyd—looking, Emmy said, like the lunacy side of genius—held them up, one by one, asked us to name them, gave us a word of approbation or more often correction, and then delivered a short lecture on each, as though rehearsing for a more important occasion. Mamma was the only one polite enough to appear interested. Julia said afterwards she could only have borne it if he had been thrice his age; but it was Emmy who penetrated even his hebetude, an act which cost her his displeasure for some days to come during which he refused to speak to her. He held up the painting of a Christmas rose (Hellebore) with the remark that he was quite sure none of us knew its classical name. 'I do,' Emmy wickedly replied, 'Hell-of-a-bore, of course.'

He repeated the same banalities so often they became formalities. Each time he saw us sewing at Julia's trousseau, and in the month between our homecoming and her marriage he rarely saw us doing anything else, he said, with jocose reproof, 'A bonny bride's soon buskit, you know,' which never failed to irritate Emmy.

So occupied were our fingers with tarlatan, nunsveiling, muslin and pongee silk, with frills and tucks, smocking and gussets, that we were scarcely ever able to go out for our walks, and spring stole upon us almost unnoticed with shedded sheaths and unfolding buds.

The afternoon before the wedding the three of us, accompanied by Mr Boyd, of whom sometimes we could not be rid, went to visit the church. A man was sowing in a field on the opposite side of the loch, scattering wide the dusty grain, and I thought that we sowed now as they sowed in Biblical days; it is the reaping that is different. We went into the church to see that everything was in readiness for to-morrow's ceremony, and they left me there to wait with a message for the beadle.

It was a small church with three galleries reached by outside stairs, their stone steps hollowed by countless feet passing up and down. To fill in the time until the beadle came, I stole up to the middle gallery, which belonged to the Marquis of Mhoreneck, but he and his family came seldom now to Gel Castle and so were rarely seen in the church. When they found the sermon over-long, they could retire into a small waiting-room, adjoining the gallery, where the Kuld arms were engraved above the fireplace and the prune-coloured silk on the chairs was cut by age into shreds. There were two doors into the gallery, one for the Marquis's family

and the other for his servants. I pushed open the Marquis's
door and sat in the front pew, wondering what it would feel
like to be Lady Jane Kuld.

I had never before been alone in a church and as I sat
there, my eyes half closed, the faint smell of must from
old Bibles in my nostrils, there seemed to beat against the
drums of my ears in the silence, like the wings of invisible
birds, all the supplications, broken with inward ejaculation,
that had passed heavenwards through communing lips in
that building. Like the strong flame of a candle they were
borne upwards, as though pulled, and I, ringed round with
prayer, was caught as if into a procession. For a minute that
quivered into an eternity, we flickered, as though awaiting
admission.

The church, which had seemed to contract round me,
spread into its shadowed normal size; I saw through the
dimness the pews, which had all dwindled into the one
where I sat, ranged in dark vacant rows below me; and the
pointed windows, screened with ivy, were no longer merely
slits. Beyond them I heard the familiar wind feeling round
the church and fumbling at the door; it haunted my mind,
disturbing me with unrecalled memories of other days.

We were all three so excited that night, I felt sure none
of us would be able to sleep, as we laughed and talked
together in the bedroom where a moth or daddy-long-legs
bumped itself against the loosely papered roof. Emmy was
running about the room in her bridesmaid's dress, which
she was trying on for the last time, and which she had
carefully avoided showing papa, for it was a pale lavender,
sprigged with tiny rosebuds, and she had the feeling he
would not deem it suitable for a church service. She was
saying what a pity it was in our house you could only see
yourself in bits, while Julia sat before the mirror combing
her hair.

'I do hope,' Julia remarked, 'Mr Urquhart will be prepared to take the service to-morrow if papa feels too unwell,
for somehow I should not feel properly married if the vows
were joined by Mr Boyd.'

She was speaking quite gaily, when suddenly, without warning, she leant her forehead on the dressing-table and burst into tears.

I felt I would have done anything in this world to escape from that broken weeping, those gasping breaths between her sobs. I have never seen her cry since.

I awoke next morning to hear the cuckoo for the first time that year. On bare feet I stole to the window to discover what kind of day Julia was to have and saw the early sun tipping the topmost branches of the trees, transfiguring them into unfamiliar spirits. When I went back to bed and fell asleep again, my dreams were full of cuckoo cries.

For the last few days the house had been upside-down, with nothing in its right place, a state of affairs Emmy and I thoroughly enjoyed; the very table at which we had our meals was changed, for another leaf had been added that it could accommodate the extra company.

Mamma's youngest and favourite brother, Uncle Octavious, arrived at the manse the day before the wedding, for he was to give Julia away. He was a tall, good-looking, ponderous man, full of worldly wisdom. Emmy was his favourite and so he teased her most, telling her she had her mother's maddening habit of saying 'you know' when she knew quite well you didn't know at all. He had offended mamma deeply when we were children by saying he saw far more promise of intelligence in his puppies than in any of her babies. He had none of his sister's persuasive charm, and always said exactly what he thought, whether it happened to be popular or not.

I think it was from him Emmy inherited her uncompromising attitude. Julia was desirous to win and please but Emmy made no effort to enslave any one. She always was what she thought. If she felt disapproving, she made her disapproval clear; people had either to take her or leave her for what she was—herself.

We all rose early that morning except Uncle Octavious,

who was more untethered by time than any one I have
ever met. He refused to be hurried over his scandalously
late breakfast, although Julia warned him she would never
forgive him if he kept her waiting.

'There's plenty of time for my breakfast and your wedding,' he informed her, 'as I'm sure Drake would tell
you. You know, our whole lives consist of this kind of
thing—seeing things out of proportion. Think of the
furore and fever we worked ourselves into last year over
something that now leaves us quite cold.'

'I hope it will take more than a year for my marriage to
leave me cold,' Julia rejoined.

'You never know,' he replied lugubriously, 'for after
all love is merely seeing the loved one hopelessly out of
proportion. Then, you'll find, you'll both waken up one day
to the fact that the other is quite ordinary and is peopling
the world in hundreds. That's why I never married,' he
added complacently, 'I always knew I would be the first
to waken up.'

He was ready in plenty of time despite his talk and we
beguiled him with flattering words to do exactly what we
wanted. 'Really, Uncle Octavious,' Julia protested, 'it's
more like your reception than my wedding.' 'You don't
mean it,' he informed her heavily, 'but it's nice to hear
you all the same. Now you must forget to be dominant for
once and stand where I put you when we're in the church,
or I shall be giving Emmy away to poor Mr Strathern.'

When we walked from the manse to the church, under
the trees clad in ivy, we made so unusual a procession that
I felt as unreal and removed from my everyday self as if we
were all strangers. The day was dull with a promise of sun
on lightened mountain top and moving loch. The church
looked very old that morning, as though at the first breath
of wind or slightest subsidence it would crumble into dust.

Within, the pews were filled by rows of faces, although
it was a very quiet wedding, for all papa's parish had
come to see Julia married. Papa was waiting to perform
the ceremony. I remember thinking he could not be well,

for his face wore an unhealthy purplish look, like the bloom of a grape. Edwin Strathern—I never grew quite accustomed to calling him merely Edwin—stood there, upright and military-looking—like a soldier awaiting execution, Uncle Octavious told Julia afterwards.

She was almost as tall as the two tall men she stood between in her parchment coloured dress which was so stiff it could stand by itself. Her face looked pale in the gloom of the church, so that she stood, with her looped hair and her hands idle at her sides, like a vital figure of long ago from which time has drained all colour.

I have a memory of Emmy's face, resolute and ardent, of the tall fastidious Nicholas seeming very near me, of the ferryman at the back of the church, his cadaverous face, with eyes lost in deep channels, looking like an unlit Hallowe'en lantern, and of little Morag MacDiarmid, the shepherd's daughter, her hair yellow as straw, nodding her head on its long stalk of a neck.

The sun, its brightness penetrating into the shadiest places in the wood as it filtered through the thick undergrowth, suddenly flooded the church, entering it like a separate presence. We blinked in its dazzling light as we made our way back to the manse and mamma, whose eyes kept swilling with tears, cried out to Julia, ' "Happy is the bride the sun shines on," my darling!'

Papa, who was feeling the strain, went to bed immediately after the ceremony. Julia bade him good-bye in his room a couple of hours later and kissed mamma at the door. Then we all, members of both families, saw the bride and bridegroom into the carriage waiting for them at the gate, where the horses impatiently pawed the ground. Even the coachmen looked festive with favours and button-holes.

Everything seemed living at its most intense that afternoon, from the stormy sky to the trees with their boles so vividly green-stained, from the wry earth turned by the plough to Julia, buttoning and unbuttoning her long, violet-coloured gloves as she stood beside Edwin, her lips smiling, saying good-bye. The very shadows flung across the gleaming carriage were deepened into meaning.

I knew with Julia's departure something would leave my life never to return in the old intimate way, some one dependable, who let one lean on her and who had always taken her 'darg'. I could not bring myself to look at her as I kissed her good-bye.

She leant precariously far out of the window, and waved to us. And suddenly I knew at that moment, made frantic with parting, that only Emmy and I were real to her. I felt she was still waving to us long after the carriage had turned the corner.

*Book Four*

'Do you think it's wrong to want something you know you can't have?' Emmy asked me one day as we sat in a small enclosed place she had discovered, high on the bank of the burn.

'Nannie would say it was,' I replied dubiously, feeling the question was too weighty to answer on my own authority.

'Oh, Nannie—Nannie's idea of life is to want nothing and you'll never tempt Providence to send you nothing. But what happens when you can't help yourself from wanting something although you don't want yourself to want it? After all, I never asked, I never wanted to fall in love with him.'

I had been watching, strung on a thorn bush, a spider's web with petals of flowers and pollen caught in it, but her words startled me so I forgot everything else as I jerked my head to gaze at her.

'I was far happier before,' she continued, digging up with one hand the spongy moss at her side, 'far happier. How more than tolerably we would get on without our emotions. What, in heaven's name, are they given us for, except to waste and bewilder us? I can't think of anything now but I am thinking of him at the same time; it's as though he had stolen my mind. I don't want to go to stay with Julia; I know so well what it's going to be like. Why is heaven always so near the brink of hell? I tell you, I know to the moment when he is going to enter the room and if I am to see him or not. Even when there are miles between us, it's still the same. What can you do with yourself when you are tuned like a harp to some one else's emotions and you feel his thoughts beat through to you?'

I remembered how Nicholas Strathern on Julia's wedding-day, three months ago, had turned to look at Emmy as she came out of the manse, in her bridesmaid's frock, with Christine and Stephen Wingate.

'But, Emmy,' I said faintly, 'if you know he cares for you, isn't that all that matters? I would have thought that would mean everything in the world to you.'

'How can it mean anything but unhappiness whether I know he cares or not? How can there ever be anything but insecurity and conflict between us? On his side he is willing, "I love but I cannot say I love, so I shall pretend indifference," and on mine I am saying, "Nothing can ever come of this, so let us kill this thing between us." And I cannot kill it, it is more alive than I am. If I died to-morrow, it would still live on. If he went to the other end of the world, he would still be bound to me and I to him, his thought stepping on my thoughts and mine on his.'

In my bewilderment I thought she meant she could not marry Nicholas Strathern because he was the son of Julia's husband. Whether a woman could marry the son of her sister's husband was a point that had puzzled me and I had secretly tried to find out in a Table of Affinities in one of papa's books.

'It would be illegal then?' I asked her ponderingly, but she was not listening and I had to repeat my question.

'Illegal!' she exclaimed, looking at me, her brows drawn. 'What are you talking about? What would be illegal?'

'For you to marry Nicholas Strathern.'

'Oh, Lisbet,' she said, 'how stupid you are. Did you think I was talking about Nicholas Strathern all this time? Why, I believe that man positively dislikes me, as I certainly do him. Of course I never meant him. It was Stephen Wingate I was talking of.'

As I looked into her quivering face, something almost unbearably painful stirred in me. I could not speak but sat motionless beside her for what seemed an eternity while far below us light span in the glimmering greenness as the swiftly moving burn swept over ferns, straining on their

roots from the banks, and drenched in its floods the low-
bending branches of trees. At last Emmy stirred beside me,
straightening her frock as she rose and said:

'We had better be going now—I have my packing to
finish and Julia said the carriage would be here at four.'

She walked so quickly I had to half run to keep up with
her, and still I could not speak. I helped her to finish her
packing and strap up her bag, and asked her if she did
not think she should take her old hair brush as well as
her new and if she had remembered to pack the sash of
her lilac dress.

After she was gone, I did not think of her; I felt I was
not strengthened yet to contemplate what she had told me.
Instead I sat in the parlour trying to concentrate all my
powers on what mamma was saying in an effort to blot out
everything else, for the time being, from my memory. But
I think while she was speaking my mind must have gone
blank for a moment, for I became aware of her voice bearing
to me as though from a far distance, like a voice that comes
from the sun and takes years on its journey. I looked at her
as if seeing her for the first time after many days as she sat
pleating her sewing between her fingers to crease it into a
hem while she remarked what a pity it was papa was always
so unreasonable when he was ill. Suddenly I wondered what
she really thought within herself, what ships sailed into her
harbour when she sat alone. 'I suppose it is old-fashioned
now,' I heard her saying, referring to a footstool Julia had
been offered for her new home and which she had refused,
'it's the new beaded fender-stools they like now, Julia says.
Your Aunt Fanny sewed it, you know—the only thing
poor Fanny ever finished. Perhaps Emmy might like it one
day, or you, dear—I would like you to have it.' She was
threading her needle but she dropped her hands before the
thread, stiffened with wax, found the eye. I think for the first
time she was startled at the thought of the three souls she
had sent journeying into the world.

Papa was still unwell, so that, with Mr Boyd, only three
of us sat at table that evening. He always supplied a more

or less constant flow of conversation; I would have more patience with him now, but in those days his inanities and repetitions filled me with a weariness I probably did not take sufficient pains to conceal. That day, as he pattered on, asking questions although not seeming to do so, for he had an insatiable curiosity, and discoursing at length on our answers, I felt pent up to the point of screaming.

'You will be quite bereft without Miss Emily, Miss Lisbet. We must find some little ploys to keep you from wearying. And then it will be your time to visit Mrs Strathern and Miss Emily's to be the odd one. I suppose it will be inclination that prompts Mrs Strathern to invite you singly, for I presume if her house is large enough to accommodate one sister, it will be large enough to accommodate two at the one time. What is that, Mrs Lockhart? Indeed—large enough for the whole family? A beautiful house? Well, well, I'm sure it will be. And then it will be your time to visit your daughter and we shall all have to set to to console Mr Lockhart in your absence—'

That night, before lighting the candle, I stood for long at our bedroom window. I was seeing the world distorted then through lobes of tears, and the trees outside seemed livid things to me, fretted and frayed with winds and knurred with age.

Although Julia's country home was only eight miles distant from the manse, we saw practically nothing of her or the Stratherns while Emmy was on her first visit, which lasted a month. I was waiting for her at the manse gate on the afternoon we expected her home. She descended from the carriage in a new bonnet and holding high in one hand a covered bird-cage.

'Oh, Lisbet,' she said, 'it is good to see you again. Yes, Julia gave me the bonnet—she wanted me to have pink ribbons but I thought cherry were more uncommon.'

'And a bird, Emmy—oh, how lovely. I hope it's a singing one. Let me see it—do let me see it.'

'It's a canary with a green breast. It was chirping away to me all the time in the carriage while I held the cage on my knee. Lisbet, don't ask me in front of any one who gave it to me, and I'll tell you all about it later when we are alone.'

The opportunity of being alone together did not come until bed-time, for after supper mamma, who wanted to hear all the news, sat with us while Emmy unpacked. But once we were in the bedroom alone for the night, and while I brushed my hair, Emmy gave me details about her stay which she could not give mamma. She lay in bed with her hands clasped behind her head, each pointed arm looking like a little white wing.

'Did you see anything of any one besides the Stratherns?' I asked falteringly.

'I saw him twice,' she replied, coming to the point with disconcerting suddenness; there were no half measures with Emmy. 'He arrived to stay with his aunt a few days before I left. The day before yesterday Julia and Christine

and I called on his mother, who was visiting her sister with
Stephen.'

'And what is she like?'

'Very small and very fragile and everything about her very
beautiful. Lisbet, wasn't it odd, she didn't like me. I don't
mean that not liking me is odd but it was strange that almost
at first sight I felt disapproval of me massing round her.'

'You only imagined it.'

'No, I didn't,' she said impatiently, 'you must believe
me. I would have been only too glad to think she
was drawn to me, but even if—even in any other
circumstances—that woman would not have liked me.
I could quite believe she could even hate me.'

'Perhaps    he—Stephen—said    something—something
about you.'

'No, no, he wouldn't do that; he's lived with her all his
life and must know her. Besides, what could he say? No,
she simply felt strongly antagonistic whenever she saw me,
and that's the long and the short of it.'

'And you only saw him twice?'

'Something very strange happened,' she went on, without
answering. 'The afternoon we were calling on his mother,
the talk turned on wishing-wells, and Julia said I had found
one and told me to tell them about it. I felt very foolish, for
there was really nothing to tell, only once Julia and I were
walking through a wood and, in a clearing, we came upon
a pool choked with last years' leaves. It looked very secret
lying there, hidden by all those old trees, and Julia said it
was the kind of place where a very old shrunken kelpie
might sleep and I said perhaps it was a wishing-pool. We
both knelt on the ground to wish and drink; the water was
acrid with leaf mould and seemed to rush to meet our lips.
But I couldn't tell them all that, so I merely said we had
discovered a pool in a thicket of old trees. "I know where
you mean," Stephen said, looking at me, "I found it too,
and it's a queer pool, for sometimes, no matter how hard
you search, you can't find it." That was the only time he
spoke to me directly.'

She was sitting upright in bed now, her hands clasped before her on top of the sheets.

'Well, the next afternoon Julia had visitors, not very nice ones, and I went for a walk by myself, for I wasn't feeling very happy. I was thinking if only each of us were made up of one person and not divided into two, one part always wishing and the other wondering why it should all be, one appealing and the other reasoning, and neither ever satisfied or giving you any peace. I wasn't paying much attention to where I was going, when suddenly I heard a frog croak and, between the tree-trunks, I saw the little wishing-pool. I went forward, although I don't know why, and there, on a flat stone at the pool's edge, I saw something bright in a cage. It was a canary and I think it was frightened by the place, for it kept hopping about the cage and giving little scared twitters. I picked it up and looked round, but there was no one about, so I took four sticks and made the initial E on the stone, and went away. Perhaps I shouldn't have done that; I wish I hadn't and yet I'm glad I did.'

'And did anything happen?' I asked.

'I took it back to Julia's,' she said, 'and it was only when I saw Nicholas and Julia and Edwin coming down the drive towards me that I realised I could not very well tell them how I had come by it. I grew frantic watching them nearing me and seemed to advance towards them so rapidly myself. "Why, Emmy," Julia called whenever she was within earshot, "what is that you're carrying?" "It's a bird," I said desperately, "a bird in a cage." "Did you get it from the gipsies?" Edwin asked, but before I could answer, Nicholas said, "It's a good cage—they probably stole it."'

I blew out the candle and, putting my mouth too close to it, burnt my lip.

'So heaven was with me,' Emmy finished; 'it shouldn't have been in the circumstances, I know, but it was.'

Julia had spent her honeymoon abroad and sent home by Emmy a present for each of us, including a brooch for Nannie. Nannie was like most Scotch people, a lordly giver and a most ungracious taker. We knew she would never wear the brooch but keep it for all time in her trunk beside her various other presents.

'Eh, Miss Emmy,' she said, 'Miss Julia shouldna have spent a' that guid money on me. I thocht ye would mebbe bring me back a brooch.' You could never surprise Nannie; if you told her the most startling, unforeseen news, she would exasperate you by remarking, unimpressed, 'Ay, I was expecting that.'

A few days after Emmy's return she prepared a picnic for us. We had intended to walk as far as the Cairn Jarak but it was so hot we went no farther than the ruined sheilings, stopping often on our way on the slightest pretext to try to get cool. First it was to watch the Mhoreneck to Dormay coach as it posted down the road far below us, its driver clad in his scarlet coat and tall white hat. Then it was to drink at a burn which was unsatisfactory, as Emmy said, for we managed to swallow very little water and thoroughly wet our hair and faces, which we dried on our petticoats. We had an argument about something, whose turn it was to carry the basket with the eatables, I think, and by the time we reached the sheilings were at the stage when Emmy was provoking and I had become sedate.

The sheilings had been built amongst the desolate hills with boulders taken from the face of the mountains and snow-white quartz brought from cloud-capped Sgur. Now only tumbled walls marked the place where the Highland women used to live throughout the summer, herding and milking the cattle that grazed on the sweet mountain grass and making butter and cheese. Weeds grew over the crumbling fanks and in the bothies could be seen blackened hearths where fires used to burn. Buried in the mouldering thatch of one of the sheilings, papa had once found a rusty sword—perhaps a relic from the days of the '45 when arms were contraband.

The drowsy drone of wild bees filled the air, laden with the mountain scents of heather and thyme, and every few minutes we heard a small cracking sound as the broom seeds burst out of their black pods with the heat of the sun.

Emmy was determined to make me laugh, which was her way of coming to terms, and I was equally determined not to give the suspicion of a smile, when I happened to look up and see, watching us over the broom bushes, a face round as an O. I was so startled I kept my mouth open and forgot to take a bite of Nannie's pancake. Mr Boyd loomed massively nearer, treading through the bushes like a bull.

'Ah,' he exclaimed, pretending to be surprised at seeing us, 'so this is where you are.'

We said that it was and Emmy remarked she was afraid we had eaten all the nicest things, as we always began the wrong way round at picnics, but there was still something in the basket. He waved away all thought of food but seated himself beside us and, removing his hat, placed it on a boulder. It had left a hot mark round his head and he took out a large white handkerchief to mop his pink brow.

The drawback to Mr Boyd was that you were no sooner beginning to like him a little better than he did or said something that made you dislike him as heartily as ever. He now turned towards me, stretching his large face into its wide, sudden smile which revealed all his teeth and never reached his eyes.

'And why a picnic to-day?' he asked. 'It is neither of your birthdays, is it?'

'No,' Emmy answered for me, 'it isn't. Nannie gave us one because it is such a beautiful day and we thought it would be something nice to do.'

Each time she moved her head suddenly, her brown curls bobbed, which somehow made her seem more alive than other people. She bent to tie her shoe-lace now and I saw him cast his glance over her; there was something in his look I could not fathom and, turning my eyes away, I wished I had not seen it.

'You are very lucky,' he said slowly, as though gathering his thoughts together, 'more lucky than you probably realise,' and he shook his head as if commiseration were called for. 'A time will come, you know, when you won't be able to have picnics just when you want them.'

'Then it's very wise to take full advantage when we can, isn't it?' Emmy said serenely.

He thought she was trying to be flippant and pursued carefully, as though she had not spoken.

'When you are married, for instance, you will not be able to run out of the house just when you take it into your head that you want a picnic.'

'Our husbands may like them too,' Emmy said idly, 'and run with us.'

'It is scarcely a subject to make jokes upon,' he returned so severely she looked at him in surprise; 'it is one of the most solemn undertakings of the Christian church, as you may one day discover. One is not fitting oneself for future responsibilities by exhibiting flyaway manners and saucy speech.'

'Well, well,' she said, suddenly wearied, 'there's no good trying on pinching shoes until you know if you'll have to wear them.'

'But you will have to begin to think seriously on such matters,' he insisted with irritation. 'Do you never consider that your lack of gravity, which sometimes comes very near impiety, may estrange people from you, people who are quite willing—nay, anxious—to think well of you?'

'No,' Emmy said, looking at him levelly over the basket, 'I have not. If people don't like me as I am—I'm sorry, and there's an end to it.'

There was a pause in which I watched the white clouds, sailing on an unbelievably blue sky, build themselves into shapes like the mountains below.

'None of us can expect,' he said, more pleasantly, 'every day to be a picnic. The calendar is made up of commonplace days, and after all that is best—the plain things of life are always best and last the longest.' He looked urbanely from one to the other. 'Better to be married to—shall we say?—a minister like your father, the highest calling in the world, and pass your days in the homely atmosphere of a sheltered manse than be the dupe of false excitement and worldly show, which cannot endure.'

I felt Emmy beside me let out her breath; she began to pack the cups into the basket and I leant forward to help her.

'Nothing,' he continued with the persistence of the insensitive, 'deceives the youthful so much as appearance. Good looks are, after all, merely an accident that might have happened to any one. You do not want to be liked for the comeliness of your face, which will fade all too soon and has nothing to do with you, but for the comeliness of an unpretentious nature; just as you do not want to set store and be deceived by a man's handsome exterior. "Handsome is as handsome does".'

'Oh, looks mean nothing to me,' Emmy exclaimed, rising to her feet, and I saw him, quick with interest, glance up at her. She was impishly grave. 'I have enough for two.'

He did not offer to carry the basket, which annoyed me, and on the way home, although both Emmy and I tried to bring him into the conversation, he barely replied, making it quite clear he was bending to neither of us.

The following day Julia called to see us and take me back with her for a visit. It was the first time she had been in her old home since her marriage, and I think she wondered how she had ever been able to live in it for so long and not be aware of its fadedness, squeaking doors and shadow-mottled interior. I know when we were going up the path together, she took my hand and began to run, as though trying to escape from something.

Like Emmy, I stayed with her a month. My visit was a happy one, filled with picnics, excursions and tea parties, for each day Julia planned to do something different and Edwin was always kindly. The pleasantness of the days was only disturbed by frequent crises between husband and wife which were, I grieved to see, mostly created by Julia.

There were depths of tragedy in her that her married life, with its ease and social trivialities, did not satisfy. The disputes that arose were merely the outlets for a dissatisfied temperament. Edwin liked to evade what was unpleasant, Julia exaggerated her point of view to have it recognised. And at every quarrel, which seemed to his bewilderment to mount out of nothing at all, he would throw rashly to the winds all his advantages and flounder in a sea of protests and excuses. No matter how unquestionably he was in the right, Julia, with all her ready resources of keen mind and nimble tongue, would discomfit him every time, unless she worked him into a passion.

But she could never sustain any quarrel for long and once peace was sealed for the time being, with honours unevenly distributed, there could not be found two better-humoured

people. In his high spirits and excitement, he was more
youthful than either Julia or I.

Nicholas Strathern was staying at Gel Lodge when I
arrived but left to go south a few days later. I remember so
well the afternoon he left. It was a day of glorious sunshine
with a blue, unclouded sky, and we had tea in the garden
under the trees. Julia had gone with Christine that morning to bid good-bye to Stephen Wingate, whose leave was
over, and Christine had wept ever since the parting until,
at tea-time, she had no longer any tears to cry. Her eyes,
in her little face like a baby owl's, were red and her hand
opened and shut convulsively on her handkerchief, rolled
into a wet ball. Edwin tried to coax her to eat and she did
take a little cake, while Julia, in an effort to make her think
of something pleasant, began to talk of her wedding, which
was to take place in early spring.

'It is really going to be very difficult,' Christine said tear-
fully, 'because Aunt Bertha says I *must* have Cousin Victoria
Grey for a bridesmaid but she is so tall she will dwarfen
us all. And Louise Grey has red hair which is so awkward
as what suits her doesn't suit Victoria. Then there will be
Emmy, of course, she is to be first bridesmaid whatever
Aunt Bertha says about the Greys, and Dot Brooke—'

'How she used to quarrel with Martin when we were all
small,' remarked Nicholas, 'because he would call her Carry
One.' He placed a small table beside me on which to put
my cup of tea. 'This,' he said, 'is what is called a delicate
attention. You didn't know a delicate attention looked like
a table, did you?'

He was always most charmingly attentive to me, yet once
or twice I found myself wondering if he were not slightly
amused by me as sometimes I very much feared he was.
But now I was beginning to lose my tongue-tied shyness
with him—just when he was leaving, and I felt the little
ground I had gained would be completely lost by the next
time we met.

I went to the gates with him to wave him good-bye
because he said he liked a fuss being made over him

and none of the others would go. 'Anyway, Lisbet,' he said, laughing, 'you are the one I would have chosen if I could—I would give them all for you.' As I saw their faces, idly smiling, turned towards me, I found myself wishing with a passion that terrified me that it were true.

We walked together over the lawn whose grass was smooth and dark, as though its colour had become intensified and deepened by years of constant rolling. Underneath the rhododendron bushes in the drive, we saw some pale flowers, drained of all colour, growing from the chapped earth. They were strange and unreal as flowers at night.

'We won't ask the gardener their name,' Nicholas said, 'in case we discover they are quite ordinary. They are like the spirits of flowers, aren't they, Lisbet? And now I'll have to leave you or I shall lose all my connections, but it's nice to think the next time I see you we'll be saying good-day instead of good-bye.'

Long after the carriage had driven round the corner, I waited. I felt as though I stood on the very brink of the world, for it was there, where the two noseless faces rested on the gate-posts, that Nicholas Strathern first stooped and kissed me.

I did not want to join the others yet and wandered into one of the green-houses. The heat matted the hair on my brow and blurred the glass. I brushed a space clear with my sleeve to look outside and saw the emblematic shadow of a tree thrown across the lawn. Eternity was caught between its branches. As I watched it through the rapidly misting glass, I wondered if everything on this earth were symbolic of another world, if everything, on its journey to decay, meant something. Perhaps the shadows of things were like the lives of people. The thing that threw these changing shades, which morning narrowed, noon stretched and night destroyed, remained the same. And the thing that beat within each person was still there through all their stressful unplanned lives, so stirred or distorted with passion; the only thing each could justly claim as quite his own, the changeless thing of which we go so unaware from cradle to grave.

I shut the door of the greenhouse behind me. Little ferns grew from the steps and a small-leafed ivy covered the stone grape-encrusted balustrade with its disproportionately large urn on each pillar. They were streaked at the base with a vivid green fungi, brilliant like all the colours of creeping banes: the blue bloom of mould and the scarlet or yellow mildew of plants.

Julia, shadowed under her garden hat, and Edwin were sitting alone under the trees. My feet were noiseless on the grass and as I neared, I heard them speak of Christine.

'She shouldn't cling to him so,' Julia was saying protestingly, 'it must exhaust him. She should give him breathing-space and stop dwelling on his every word as she does. Why, he can't move an inch but her eyes follow him.'

'Her feelings will probably become calmer to him once they are married,' Edwin said easily.

'More probably more intense,' responded Julia; 'it's a symptom of insecurity. She should be told that if you keep the cage door open, the bird is not nearly so likely to fly away.'

She was buttonholing and her thread had become twisted: I watched her let her needle hang to twirl it unwound.

I knew something had happened to upset Emmy whenever I saw her on the morning I returned home, but I had not the opportunity of questioning her, for I arrived only a few minutes before dinner. As the meal progressed, I began to wonder what was amiss with Mr Boyd, for he was unwontedly mute. This silence was so unnatural to him that it made me feel uneasy. Only once did he break it and that was to admonish Emmy for speaking impatiently to mamma. I thought by this time we had all grown accustomed to Mr Boyd's trying habit of giving his opinion on matters that did not concern him, but that day at dinner I saw Emmy glare at him so openly across the table that I wondered how she dared. She then repeated very sweetly her exact words to mamma, and looked coldly again at Mr Boyd, her eyebrows raised, as though demanding an explanation for his reproof. By the time we finished dinner I realised that what had upset Emmy had also caused Mr Boyd's unusual silence.

She left the room whenever the meal was over to finish placing, side by side, the cool stone jars of this year's jam in the cupboard in the hall. I heard her call to me to come and see how nice it looked. Mr Boyd followed me from the parlour and, without speaking to us as he passed, took his black hat and stick from the stand. For some seconds he stood with his back to us, his neck rolled above his collar, evidently debating whether or not he should take his coat. We saw him struggle into it and felt the house shake as he closed the door heavily behind him.

'Emmy,' I asked wonderingly, looking at the shut hall door, 'whatever is the matter with Mr Boyd?'

Her face flushed deeply, as though at some uncomfortable recollection. 'Oh, Lisbet,' she said, 'I do hope papa will be well soon. Nothing has gone right since that man has come. The very house feels different when he's in it.'

'But what has happened, Emmy?' I asked.

'The day before yesterday I was setting the flowers for mamma. Ever since you went he's been strange, Lisbet. I can't describe it, but he seemed to be what he would think was being nice to me, and I don't know why, but I hated it. There's something wrong about that man, Lisbet; I am sure he has all the wrong thoughts. I knew as well as though I read it on a page before me that he wanted to speak with me alone, and I was determined he wouldn't. Somehow I didn't want to hear what he was going to say. You've no idea how difficult it was, Lisbet, for it wasn't as though you were at home. All my walks were spoiled, getting out of the house without his knowing and becoming breathless with hurry in case he was following. Do you know, even in the bedroom at night—I know it was silly and ridiculous—I kept looking round in a fright, thinking he was there. Well, the day before yesterday, I thought he had gone out—you know how regularly he takes his morning walk on other days, and I was setting the flowers for mamma alone in the parlour. I saw the door open and the next moment he put in his face to see if I were there. I knew he had caught me, for mamma was making papa's bed with Nannie and wouldn't be down for some time, but I went on snipping the flower stems as though nothing untoward were happening. I heard him say something that sounded very foolish about flowers and me, and the next thing I knew was that he was standing over me. He always seems to have so much face, and he came so near me that when I looked up I saw the network of tiny purple veins on his cheeks. I began to feel stifled, as though some one had lifted a flap of the carpet and filled my nose with dust. I felt he was trapping me and I wanted to run to the ends of the world from him, but he was like a wall before me. I knew he was going to propose and I felt I would do anything—anything—to stop him. I

didn't want to be borne down on and I felt if he kissed me
I would be sick. I must have gone quite cold, for he took
my hand and exclaimed it was like ice. I think he was quite
enjoying the effect he saw he had on me. He said something
about some one needing to take care of me. I knew what was
coming, so I said to save his feelings and to give him a way
out, "No, no, I don't need any one to do that." He came still
nearer, if that were possible, and said something about my
not knowing my own mind. I grew desperate then and said,
"That's the one thing I do know, Mr Boyd. I don't want
to marry any one and would have to say no should any one
ask me." I wanted to make it clear I wouldn't marry him
before he actually asked me, for I knew he could never
bear it otherwise: he is such a preposterous man who sees
everything out of proportion, particularly himself.'

'And what did he say then, Emmy?'

'He dropped my hand as though it had been fire. He
didn't say anything for a few minutes but he recovered himself astonishingly quickly, Lisbet. By the time he reached
the door he was himself again, very red in the face but
bristling with a terrible kind of laboured sarcasm. He stood
moving up and down on his heels, you know the habit he's
got, and said, "So you are not going to marry? No, I don't
think you ever will, for I don't suppose any one rich enough
or handsome enough for you will ever come your way.
And why, may I ask, do you make me your confidant?"
I didn't answer, of course, for I knew he was trying to
save himself by taking advantage of my being like Nancy
Baxter and refusing the man before he axed her. If that's
any consolation to him, he's quite welcome to it as far as
I am concerned.'

'You were quite right, Emmy,' I said hotly. 'And what
was he like to you—afterwards?'

'Oh, unbearable. He never even says "good-morning"
to me now and only speaks to me to censure me—you
saw what he was like at dinner—as though he were my
schoolmaster and wanted to lower me before the class. I do
hate rudeness. I won't sit in the same room with him unless

some one else is there; but I don't know what it is about him, he seems to overflow the house.'

She stood looking down at me from the kitchen chair. There was a clarity about her face, for her thoughts did not conflict; everything she said sprang from what she herself considered and was in no way prompted by or adjusted to what was expected of her. Her directness of speech and vividness of colouring, the brightness of her eyes, her brown hair dusted with gold, the delicately marked eyebrows, which gave a proud look to her face whether she willed it or not, all served to counteract the impression of extreme fragility which her very fine skin might have imparted.

She folded up the duster and carried the chair she had been standing on back to the kitchen. Mr Boyd, who was visiting some people on the other side of the loch, did not return until late that night. The house seemed to become ours again in his absence. As we sat at tea, we could hear in the distance the rumbling of the carts returning from the fields to Gow Farm. The afternoon sunshine shone brightly and the yellow leaves came raining down; their shadows poised and fluttered on floor and wall until one almost thought the leaves themselves were imprisoned in the rooms.

I lay awake that night after Emmy had fallen asleep, letting the familiar room and house gather round me again as though I had never left it. I heard Nannie rake out the kitchen fire before going to bed; the sound reached me as though from the bottom of a deep well and I, beginning to be rocked with sleep, took long to connect it with Nannie, the kitchen and myself. I heard Mr Boyd come in and lock up the door. After that, the house settled itself for the night, a shelter of silence cut off with mist, bounded by rain and cradled in winds.

When Emmy caught a quinsy, Nannie said January had always been an unlucky month for Lockharts and Royalty. I sat beside her most of the day, talking and reading out to her, but time went by heavily in the room where the skylight cast a square of light on the floor. Emmy could no longer harness her mind by throwing herself into activity; and now her hands were idle, her unchecked thoughts had her at their mercy. I think during those days she knew melancholy in all its myriad forms, from depression of the body to sadness of the spirit, from haunting mournfulness to flagging lassitude and desolating despondency. But she never spoke even to me of what she thought or felt.

Edwin sent her a beautiful bunch of black grapes and she sat up in bed under the sloping ceiling, a shawl over her pointed shoulders, while she skinned and removed the pips of each grape. She informed me she was not going to allow herself to eat one until she had prepared them all. But after she had finished, she said they somehow did not taste so nice. 'There's a moral to that somewhere,' she remarked as she lay down again, 'but I'm too tired to think it out just now.'

Julia had spent Christmas in her Glasgow home but she returned to Gel Lodge towards the end of February, for Christine was to be married from there in spring. Julia wanted Emmy to stay with them but Emmy would not leave home, because of her throat, she said, although I knew it was quite well again. She was worn out and had no desire for her emotions to be stirred, so that she would not go even for the day to Gel Lodge for fear she should meet Stephen Wingate, but I went one afternoon in March to spend the night.

Everything was in an upheaval because of the approaching wedding, yet there seemed a lack of spontaneity and eagerness in the air. Martin was the only person who appeared to be in excellent spirits, fooling as usual at tea and making me laugh in spite of myself. But at the back of my mind lay the knowledge, realised only at that moment, that Christine's wedding was now not even a matter of weeks distant, but of days.

It was well Emmy had not come with me for Stephen Wingate had travelled north the previous day to stay with his aunt until his marriage. He was not expecting to see me that afternoon at Gel Lodge and when he caught sight of me I thought he was going to exclaim. He did not, however, but glanced round the room a little wildly, his lips parted, as though looking for some one. He stood behind me, the last place I like people to stand, with his hands on the back of my chair, and the thought streaked through my mind that, if the opportunity came, he would bend down and ask me something—I knew not what. Perhaps he, too, was not quite sure.

That was the first time I had met him since Emmy had spoken of him to me last summer on the bank of the burn, and I looked at him now as though I had never seen him before. I had always thought of him as a frank, good-looking young man with his gay blue eyes and unforced laugh. Now I had to revise that impression. This man, who stood listening to Martin's chatter yet seemed dwelling on his own thoughts, was not so tolerant as I had imagined. His blue eyes could darken, he might be moody, and I saw from a certain mettled imperiousness in his bearing I had not marked before that he would bear no restraint. In this he reminded me of Emmy with her impatient gestures and her quick suspicion if any one tried to curb her. For one dangerous moment I let my imagination picture them together; then I made myself look at Christine. She was sitting drawn back in

her low chair, as though she were being out-talked, which
she certainly was by her voluble brother, while her eyes
watched Stephen Wingate appealingly. I could sense that
she irritated him and that unconsciously she knew it. She
would reproach when she should retort, advance where
she should withdraw.

I left Julia's next day and, rather to my surprise,
Christine accompanied me in the carriage. She wanted
to see Emmy, she explained, and she thought this would
be a good opportunity when she would have my company
to the manse.

I felt myself grow bitter at the thought of Christine's
marriage, but it was not altogether resentment, which I
knew to be unjust, at Christine having what Emmy might
not have, that made me feel little at ease with her. We
had never had much to say to each other; she was
Emmy's friend and evinced no interest in me. Perhaps
the things that appealed to her in Emmy were the very
things she did not possess. She was what Nannie would
call 'finger-fed'—quite unfitted for the wear and tear
of daily life.

We sat together in the carriage, each looking out of
a different window and neither making any pretence to
keep up conversation. It was a still, motionless day with a
gloom lying over everything like the bloom on fruit. This
olive-green atmosphere, a token of coming storm, made
the landscape, with trees studded here and there, look like
the background of an old Italian picture. When we drove
through Dormay, the sound of the blacksmith's hammer
on his anvil could be heard down the length of the street.

As we neared the manse, I became conscious that
Christine's customary quietness when she was alone with
me could not account for her unbroken silence now. I stole
a look at her as she sat with her hands in her muff and saw
from her face, half turned towards the window, that she
was sunk so deep in her own thoughts she had forgotten
all about me. I wondered why she had been so anxious to
come to the manse that afternoon, nearly weeping when

Julia suggested she should wait until Monday and accompany her when she was coming to spend the whole day with us.

Emmy was waiting at the gate for me and was obviously surprised when she saw Christine. But Christine was not in the mood to notice, or care if she did, what effect her unheralded visit had. She kissed Emmy warmly, clinging to her hands and exclaiming her name as though she had at last found her.

We had tea with mamma, who spoke to Christine of her coming wedding with all her wonted enthusiasm, but Christine remained sweetly smiling and monosyllabic, her fingers plucking at her frock. After tea, she surprised me by proposing—for she usually left suggestions to others—that a walk would be very nice, and on our way upstairs for our bonnets, she put her arm through Emmy's. We had no sooner entered our bedroom when she said:

'Let's stay here for a little.'

'Yes, of course—if you want to,' Emmy agreed, 'but I hope you won't find it cold, Christine. Lisbet, shut the skylight. It's nice and undisturbed here,' she said, sitting on our bed and looking round.

Christine sat down beside her, her wide skirts making an island round her. She moistened her lips and turned her pale face beseechingly towards Emmy.

'Oh, Emmy,' she said, 'you're the only person I can tell—Juley's different somehow and I couldn't tell Aunt Bertha.'

'Tell, Christine?' asked Emmy, her face setting and her voice sharp with dread.

'About Stephen. When he's with me now it's all so different to what it used to be, and when he's away his letters are merely notes in answer to mine, with very little beginning or end.' She made a choking sound in her throat. 'I've felt a change in him ever since last summer—ever since Juley's wedding really. It's almost as though he didn't care the same. But that can't be, that can't be—I'm just the same as when he knew me first. What would you do if you were me? You're so strong and decisive and not like me who can't make up my mind or keep it fixed for two minutes on end. Say something to me. Tell me you think he cares the same as he ever did.'

Emmy's mouth dragged.

'Oh, I know what you would do,' Christine said, covering her face with her hands, 'don't say what you would do. I couldn't do that—I'm not you. Besides he might tell me that he—that he—' She began to cry behind her hands. 'I could bear anything but that, anything in the world but that. Perhaps it's only his way, perhaps all men are like that when they grow more accustomed to you. But I used to think he couldn't be anything other than gentle or say an unkind word, and now sometimes I catch him looking at me in such a curious way that makes my blood freeze. And once or twice, when he hasn't quite caught what I've said, he's spoken to me almost angrily. Emmy, you've met him and you know people even if you've only seen them once. You don't think he could be cruel, do you? Lately I've wondered when I've looked at his face. But the terrible thing is that even if I knew he were and a hundred other things besides, I would still love him and want him. What should I do? Tell me what I should do.'

'I can't think what you can do.'

'He's worked me into such a state now that I can hardly speak to him or bear to hear him speak for fear of what he'll say. I can't endure it any longer. Emmy, Emmy, tell me how I can put things right. There must be some way, there must. He cared before—at the beginning—so why shouldn't he care again? Help me, Emmy, help me.'

'If you couldn't ask him and straighten out things yourself, there's your father. He would be understanding and do anything to help you.'

'No, no, that would never do—it would be so much easier for him to tell papa than to tell—' She broke off and stared a little stupidly in front of her, as though her mind refused to comprehend what her lips said.

She began to cry soon after, forlorn sobs that shook her shoulders. Emmy, who had been leaning against the bolster as though she were very tired, knelt beside her and tried to comfort her, but Christine cried as if her heart would break. Her tears must have brought her some relief, however, for when she began to dry her eyes she seemed a little heartened.

'I may be imagining it all,' she said gaspily. 'You can imagine all kinds of things, can't you? After all, our wedding isn't so very far away.'

'No,' Emmy agreed, 'it's within a few days.'

'Seven days exactly to-day,' said Christine, winding her bonnet strings round and round her fingers; 'nothing very much could happen within that time, could it?' She stood up and we smoothed out her crumpled frock. 'Seven days!' she exclaimed, her face brightening, 'seven's a lucky number, isn't it?'

Papa had always insisted we should be sitting in church twenty minutes before the service began. The day after Christine visited us was a Sunday and, although he was still too unwell to preach, Emmy and I left the house at the usual time. We had been sitting for some ten minutes, watching the silent people in their Sabbath blacks file into the pews, when mamma entered. Although she was early, she was 'late' according to papa and arrived, as she always did, in a flurry of unbuttoned gloves and awry cape. Twenty-five years of living with papa and next a church had not yet taught her to be in time.

We moved down the pew to make room for her and she settled herself beside us. The musty odour of camphor rose from behind us where the Gow Farm children sat, sticking to their seats in the heat. The silence of the church was broken by inarticulate sounds: the pattering of the sheep-dogs' paws as they followed their heavy-booted masters into church, the creaking of pews as people took their seats, the chink of a penny laid alongside a Bible, deep breathings and the cracking of joints.

I was watching old Mrs MacDiarmid take her Bible out of its elastic strap which she snapped on to her wrist, when I realised something had happened to Emmy. It was not that she started, or tried in any way to catch my attention: I was aware only of a certain rigidity in her attitude, as though she were petrified.

She continued to sit with her gloved fingers pressing against one another in her lap, and my gaze ranged the pews to discover whom or what had such an effect upon her, but could find no answer in the faces of the crofters and their families. Then I noticed a stranger sitting in the back pew under the Dripps gallery; I had to suppress an exclamation when I saw it was Stephen Wingate.

A dozen fully-formed conjectures leapt into my mind in an instant. I waited, fully expecting others to join him, Christine or Martin, Edwin, even his mother, as though they would explain, give reason for, his presence there; but by the time Mr Boyd ascended the pulpit, he still sat in the empty pew and I knew he had come alone.

There was brilliant sunshine outside, so brilliant it was able to penetrate through the ivy-covered windows. Once inside, the glimmering light, divorced from its parent sun, seemed to shine in the dark church with a pale luminosity of its own. It washed over the rows of upturned faces, all gazing in the one direction—all except a young man staring intently from a shadowed pew.

I heard nothing of Mr Boyd's sermon that morning. His voice reverberated in my ears but I did not comprehend what it said. It exasperated me after a time, for it was like knockings on a door one does not intend to answer, and seemed to hold forth interminably.

The thump, thump of the sheep-dogs' tails on the floor told me the Benediction was being pronounced. We rose stiffly from our seat and, Emmy and I on either side of mamma, walked the few yards from the church to the manse. Emmy escaped immediately to our bedroom. I was following her when papa called me into his room to tell me to return to church and collect some papers Mr Boyd had forgotten to bring him the day before. It was inconvenient but I did as I was bid.

No sooner had I stepped outside the garden when some one moved beside a tree and I saw Stephen Wingate approach me.

'Are you from your sister?' he questioned eagerly.

'No,' I replied, 'I am to fetch some papers from the vestry for papa.'

I saw him swallow.

'Will you tell your sister I'm here?' he said after a pause.

I hesitated before I answered dubiously, 'She knows you're here—she saw you in church this morning.'

'I know she did, but will you tell her I'm still here?'

I did not know what to do, so made no reply as I looked up into his troubled face. The position he was in was so foreign and false to his character and temperament that I could imagine any one I knew fitting it better than he. He was like an unsuspecting person caught unawares in a trap of circumstance.

I ran past him on the way back from church, hating myself for the knowledge that he was in my power. Mr Boyd was in the hall when I entered and I thrust the papers into his hands to give to papa while I ran upstairs to Emmy. A few minutes later, when the house was quiet, I came downstairs again and went outside.

Stephen was standing where I had left him.

'Emmy says,' I began dutifully, 'that she wonders why you're here.'

'Tell Emmy,' he returned grimly, 'that she knows as well as I do.'

'She says,' I pursued, 'that you had better come in now you're here, but you must never come again.'

I turned on my heel, expecting him to follow me, when I felt him catch hold of my wrist.

'Miss Lockhart,' he said hoarsely, 'what would you do if you were me?'

I did not look at him as I replied:

'Not what you are doing now.'

'I know it's wrong to come like this,' he said, 'I know it is. But I had to see her even if I didn't speak.'

I took him into the parlour where mamma sat and left him to make his own excuses and explanations. Her suspicions were in no way aroused; she saw nothing odd in his sudden appearance at a far-away Sabbath service and was content to believe that his arrival was due to a vague interest in old churches. He was so linked with Christine in her mind that she never dreamed of connecting him with either Emmy or me, but, perhaps because I knew everything and therefore was highly sensitised, I was aware at dinner of Mr Boyd's unspoken comment and inward pondering. I did not then take him into serious account, however, and was grateful for the fact that papa was having his meals in his room.

After dinner we all sat in the parlour until Stephen rose to go. Emmy and I went together with him to the door where he took her hand in his.

'Good-bye,' he said. It was all he could think of saying.

Rain pricked the pane in the parlour where we sat waiting for Julia. We expected her to arrive between ten and eleven o'clock and listened for her carriage wheels on the road beyond to tell us of her approach. When she did not come by twelve o'clock, mamma remarked that she was late. Nannie waited dinner for her until one, when she brought it in. We ate it rather silently, hoping nothing was wrong, for Julia was so punctilious that we knew, if she were late, something unforeseen had happened.

When two o'clock arrived, Mr Boyd, before leaving the room, gave us his opinion that she had forgotten to come. We all sprang at him with indignant refutations, especially mamma, who, by this time, had fretted herself into the positive belief that Julia had been taken seriously ill. She began to write a letter to Edwin, which she intended to entrust to the shepherd who was going west that afternoon with some sheep, when we heard Nannie give an exclamatory greeting and Julia's voice in the hall.

She entered the room a minute later and stood with her hands leaning on the table. She was wearing a new Paisley shawl, patterned in the shades of autumn leaves, and I noticed her face was flushed.

'I'm so sorry I'm late, mamma,' she said, 'but I really could not help it, and I won't be able to wait long. Something so painful has happened. Just before I set out to come here, Stephen Wingate called to see Edwin. He wants to break off his engagement to Christine.'

I did not look at Emmy but I knew her eyes were shut as she stood with her back pressed against the wall. Mamma was the first to speak.

'Oh, never,' she said blankly. 'It would be too cruel.' Her mind did not grip as of yore and her thoughts skirted the issue. 'Whatever did Edwin say?'

'Oh, mamma,' Julia cried impatiently, 'what *could* Edwin say except that he wished to God he had found out before he became engaged.'

'But, Julia, surely—he must have given some reason.'

'He wouldn't give any reason beyond saying that his feelings had changed. Edwin asked him if there were any one else, and he wouldn't answer. He did say, of course, as he was bound to say, that he would tell Christine himself, but Edwin wouldn't permit that.'

'But he's such a nice young man,' mamma protested, 'and she's very sweet, I'm sure. Why should he break it off? And so near their wedding-day too, which makes it all the worse. There must be some one else he cares for, unless it is his mother— He's an only son, isn't he?'

'It has nothing to do with her. He admitted to Edwin, when Edwin asked him, that he hadn't even told his mother yet. Of course, I never liked that man.'

'Why not?'

Emmy's voice sounded so harsh that it was a second before I or any one else in the room connected it with her.

'Why not?' asked Julia. 'Why not? Well, I suppose I saw through him.'

'In what way?'

'Well, really, Emmy, in the same way that you see through most people—you are suspicious of what they are about to do.'

'And what do you think of what he's done?'

'I can't say very highly.'

'If you had become engaged to him and his feelings changed, you would rather he married you than told you?'

'Good heavens, no; but Christine would.'

'That's not the point. The point is that what Stephen Wingate has done is either right or wrong; the person to whom he was engaged makes no difference.'

'Don't look at me like that. I can't help it. I've had nothing to do with it.'

'But isn't it?'

'Isn't what?'

'Isn't it either right or wrong to break off your engagement when your feelings change?'

'I've not got an impersonal brain like you, Emmy.'

'It has nothing to do with impersonal brains. It has to do with right and wrong.' She began to tremble.

'I'm not Stephen Wingate's accuser, nor am I his defender. His own conscience will tell him whether he's done right or wrong.'

'You were accusing him just now.'

'I was accusing him no more than you were defending him, Emmy.'

'That's a lie.'

'Emmy, don't,' mamma cried.

'Say you don't like him now after this has happened, but don't say now you never liked him, for it isn't true and you are merely deceiving yourself.'

Julia stood gazing fixedly across the table at Emmy's face.

'I'll tell you one thing,' she said slowly, after a long pause, 'that man and his emotions are not to be depended upon. He's shown that clearly. If he can do this kind of thing once, he can do it again.'

Emmy's lips were drawn into a thin white line across her face. Her words came through them deliberately, as though forced.

'If you think that's a warning, I fling it back at you for what it's worth.'

Julia went over to her and tried to take her hands, but Emmy put them behind her back and stood rigid and withdrawn, as though if she were touched she would pass through the wall.

'Emmy, darling,' Julia said caressingly, 'what is the matter with you? You know I would hurt any one on this earth rather than you.'

'I only know I don't want to see you or speak to you.'

'But, Emmy, that's cruel. What have I done? It's not my fault. I can't be blamed for what's happened.'

'You are the last who'll be blamed.'

'Now you are being sarcastic. I don't know what to make of you. Lisbet! Mamma! I've done nothing wrong, have I?'

She had to leave within the hour after vainly trying to make it up with Emmy, who was sheathed in an hostility that warded off all approach. I went with Julia to her carriage and she beseeched my understanding and sympathy, but I was very near tears and could only wring my hands and say:

'You shouldn't have said what you did, Julia; oh, you know you shouldn't. You should have seen from her face what was happening.'

She drove away and I ran back to the manse. When I entered, I heard mamma cry out in sudden agitation:

'My darling, my darling, what is the matter? You're ill. Emmy—'

I went into the parlour and saw Mr Boyd bending over Emmy, who had evidently stumbled.

'It's nothing—it's nothing,' she said desperately. 'Don't fuss me, mamma. My bodice is too tight, that's all.' She tugged at it weakly with her hand.

'You are so white. Where are the smelling-salts? Nannie! Nannie! do you know where the smelling-salts are?'

Nannie found the smelling-salts, which no one ever used, at the foot of mamma's work-basket, but Emmy refused to have anything to do with them. I followed her upstairs and was shutting the door when I heard Mr Boyd in the hall below saying loudly to mamma that her daughter should have been *made* to smell the salts.

It was Tuesday, the day after Julia had told us of Christine's broken engagement, and Emmy had not yet spoken about it to me. I was sitting at the window threading my jumbleberry beads and she was practising at the piano. Her touch was sure and I listened to her playing even her scales with a peculiar intensity, as though by releasing the notes she were giving freedom to her thoughts. Her music was the only thing which brought her complete satisfaction, for although she sewed most beautifully, she was so exacting and particular that, to all our exasperation, she usually unpicked what she had done. The bright little basket of cross-stitch flowers on her square of holland never came up to the bright little basket painted on her brain, and in her aim for perfection Emmy had to discard much.

Nannie bustled in to set the table for tea. She was growing old now and often asked me to fetch things for her, papa's tray from upstairs or rhubarb from the garden—'There's a guid wee lady.' The china chimed as she put cup on saucer, setting an extra place, for this was Mr Urquhart's day to visit us.

He was some years older than papa and lived with his only daughter. Amy Urquhart had dedicated her life to her father and took such care of him that she never permitted him to be well. For the last twenty years she had prayed that comfort and strength be given her dear papa in his fast declining years; yet approaching old age did not seem to be loosening Mr Urquhart's grip on life, while the years left his daughter faded and drained of any individual vitality.

He arrived half an hour before tea. The top part of his bald head was quite flat, so that he always reminded me of a doll whose hair has come off, and he had a habit of working his eyebrows while he was speaking, an affectation which had now grown into an unconscious characteristic. I took him upstairs before tea to see papa, whom he irritated profoundly by remarking how very well he was looking.

'I may be better, George,' papa replied, 'but I'm not right yet by any manner of means.'

'It's your colour, William, that is so excellent—'pon my soul, it's better than my own.'

'I am running a high evening temperature, of course, George.'

'Yes, yes, but I'm glad you're looking so much better.'

'Then I must be looking what I decidedly am not feeling. It will be many a long day yet, I fear, before I am very much better.'

'Still we must have "pains to have gains", William, "pains to have gains".'

Tea recalled us downstairs and we all sat round the table. Mr Urquhart had no news and was most long winded, while Mr Boyd was unusually silent, contradicting no one.

After tea I went to Gow Farm to bring back some milk for supper. Emmy would not come with me and, as there was nothing to hurry home for, I took my time, placing the jug on the stone bridge and leaning over to look at the burn below.

I watched the water course past until time lost all significance, until nothing mattered beyond those falling waters. The trees growing on the precipitous banks, the hump of the bridge, my water-widened face, it mirrored them all and flowed by, changing yet unchanged, as it would still flow by when we were no longer there.

At last I realised it had grown colder and straightened myself to go. Pins and needles pricked my hands and my elbows were sore with leaning on them for so long. Dusk, 'between-the-lights' Nannie called it, had crept amongst the trees, and across the loch Fingal rose, snow-capped, like an enchanted mountain, for its greenness was becoming obscured by a faint, smoke-like, blue haze which deepened as dark drew on.

When I reached the manse gate I saw Julia's carriage waiting outside and quickened my steps as I walked down the path. Voices were coming from the parlour when I entered and I found it was not Julia who had come, but Edwin.

'You didn't see Christine, Lisbet, did you?' mamma asked me.

'Christine?' I said vaguely. 'No, I didn't see her.'

'She's not at home,' Edwin said, 'and I thought it very probable she had come to see Emily.'

I was staring at him across the room and saw him for the first time look every year of his age.

'She wouldn't walk here,' I said, moving closer to him, 'she would take the carriage—the servants would know.'

I heard him draw his breath back between his teeth.

'The servants can tell me nothing of her,' he said, and he held my gaze with his as though to focus his thoughts.

A knocking sounded on the front door. We listened to Nannie's footsteps as she hurried from the kitchen to answer it. A man's voice was heard, then across the hall came a heavy tread, and in the doorway stood an unfamiliar coachman, his stout face quaking and sweating.

'Why, what is it?' mamma asked anxiously, and Edwin turned painfully to face the newcomer.

'Mr Strathern—I canna tell ye—I canna bear to tell ye. They've ta'en your daughter oot o' the river.'

# Book Five

I was hurrying down the road, keeping in the middle as much as possible, away from the trees, for I have a horror of bats, those mice on wings, and it was growing dark. When I reached the bridge I was startled by some one suddenly stepping from the side of the road and laying a hand on my arm.

'I didn't mean to frighten you,' said a voice. 'It's only me—Stephen Wingate. Lisbet, I must see Emmy. Should I come to the manse? Would they let me see her if I did?'

It was a moment or two before I could reply.

'You can't do that,' I said.

'Then will you tell Emmy I'm here?' he pleaded. 'Lisbet, what does she feel towards me? What do you feel? Was I wrong to do what I did? But I couldn't have gone on with it. It wouldn't have been right, marrying one woman and thinking of another, wanting her more than anything else, and if I couldn't have her, wanting no one. It would have been false to have married—false to all three of us. Oh, Lisbet, what does Emmy feel?'

'I don't know that she knows she can feel yet. You shouldn't have come so soon after—after it. You should have waited until we had all got over it more. You couldn't expect to come to the manse to-day and be greeted as if nothing had happened.'

'If you only knew—and it's not what people say and feel and make you feel, it's what your own— But you can't go on like this, there must be an end to this feeling.'

'Ah, I do know what it's been for you, but after all you are coming here to see Emmy when Christine's hardly— You should have waited for months yet until things are more smoored and don't hurt so much. Go away now and I'll tell Emmy you'll come back this time next year—'

'This time next year you'll all remember that this time last year she—'

'Well, come—write—after six months at least have passed.'

'I must see Emmy now, Lisbet, I must. You don't understand. I couldn't go without seeing her. It's asking too much of any one. I sail a week to-day. Lisbet, I must marry her before I go. Do you hear what I say?'

'You are mad—'

'If we don't marry before I go, it will never be—that I know. Have you never had convictions that are stronger than certainties? Have you never felt that everything and every one in the world and beyond the world are working against you? I tell you, I'll have her despite everything and every one, and it's got to be before I go.'

'You have to have banns cried—'

'Not always, Lisbet.'

'What good would marrying do when you are sailing next week?'

'She would be mine—she would be safe—no one could part us then.'

I felt sick and faint with apprehension.

'She couldn't do that,' I said over-emphatically, 'you know she couldn't. There's your regiment. You can't marry without—'

'I'm not a fool, Lisbet—she can come with me on the strength of the regiment. I have had permission to marry.'

'Not permission to marry Emmy, Stephen.'

'That doesn't matter—it's all the same to them, they won't know.'

'It's wrong of you to speak like this,' I told him, 'very wrong, and you will be wicked if you make any such proposals to Emmy. I won't tell her you're here because you are attempting to force things and that is bound in itself to bring disaster.'

'If you won't tell her, I'll call at the manse and that will make everything worse for every one.'

'Very well,' I said, after a pause, 'I'll tell Emmy, but,' I added without conviction, 'she will not come to see you.'

'She will come,' he said, following me in his distress, 'she will come if you tell her. She knows—I know she knows what it's been—'

Night clung like a bat to the eaves of the manse whose lights were not yet lit, but I made my way across the hall and upstairs without groping. I knew Emmy was lying down in our bedroom, for she had been having restless nights; her very exhaustion seemed to chase sleep further away and even in dreams she was astir. I heard her move as I entered; it was almost as though she had been expecting me. I told her he was waiting for her beside the bridge. She sat up in bed at my words, her hands clasped, and I caught a glimpse of her transiently lightened face, like a rain-drenched rose facing the sun. She dressed without speaking in the room pitted with shadows and I listened to her going down the stairs which creaked through the dark.

I lit the candle and straightened the bed and sat waiting for her to come back, my thoughts turning in my mind. Perhaps because I was afraid, I did not let myself think of what Stephen was saying to Emmy or she to him. Julia and Edwin had left for Glasgow that morning, and my thoughts dwelt on how grief-struck Edwin was, how powerless we were to mitigate his suffering, how bitterly Julia reproached herself for this and that, and how Emmy's upbraiding heart would not let her be. I felt like a harp whose strings have been strung to sing too many sad tunes and began to cry silently.

Nannie came into the room to blow out the candle she thought one of us had forgotten and found me sitting alone. She scolded me for catching cold and wasting a good fire downstairs. Now she was in the bedroom, she waited to take off the counterpane and fold back the bedclothes for the night.

'Nannie,' I said, and found I was shivering, 'who do you think was to blame about—about her death?'

'Na one was to blame,' she answered. 'She wasna strang enow to thole things and so ended them.'

'What should she have done, Nannie?'

'Dreed her ain dree like many a one afore her. If she had bided it would have passed like everything else. It a' passes if ye only bide lang enow.' She shook the bolster and a wan winged moth flew out.

Emmy returned just before supper and, taking off her bonnet, sat down on the edge of the bed.

'Lisbet,' she said, speaking as though it were an effort, 'he's coming to-morrow at this time and I'm to meet him under the bridge where I spoke to him to-night. How my head spins. You'll come with me to-morrow, won't you? He wants me to marry him and sail with him on Wednesday.'

'Well,' I said, 'and what are you going to do?'

A tremor passed over her face.

'I told him I would go with him.'

I could only say 'Oh' and did not look at her, but began to tidy the gloves in my opened drawer.

The following day the wind harried grey clouds across the sky and whipped the loch into waves. We left the manse when stormy twilight was beginning to fall, walking up the path between the ghostly silver stems of the birch trees. There had been a primrose sunset and its pale radiance lingered in the sky beyond the mountains still covered with snow.

At the gate we saw Mr Boyd standing, one hand on its bars, his head turned from us as though he were listening intently to something. So engrossed was he that he did not hear us approaching, for our footsteps were padded by the wet leaves that embedded the path. He started when we came up to him, as though taken aback, and held the gate open for us to pass.

'A-a-ah!' he exclaimed, recovering himself, 'shouldn't two young ladies be going home at this time instead of going out?'

'It's quite dry,' Emmy replied calmly, 'and Lisbet has a headache, so it will do her good to have the air before supper.'

'Night air will do no one good,' he responded; 'and your sister would not have headaches if she read a good deal less.'

Once round the corner, Emmy led the way. We climbed the low dyke and clambered down the steep bank of the burn, brambles clutching at our skirts. Underneath the dark bridge we stood on a small pebbly strand. It was a moss-muffled place where the wind could not strip or scathe, but moisture dripped, green gathered on the stones and spiders' webs, like cartwheels, hung. We had not been waiting long when we heard, by the snapping of twigs and steps breaking through undergrowth, Stephen approach.

'I thought I heard you coming some time ago,' he said, 'but it was only that minister man who is staying with you just now, so I walked the other way that he wouldn't see me. Emmy, darling—Emmy—'

'Oh, Stephen,' she said, and I knew she was shuddering in his arms, 'do you think a time will come when we won't remember? Now she is dead, I feel her between us as I never felt when she was alive and I thought she was going to be your wife.'

'Listen, Emmy,' he said, taking her hands, 'we must go forward. Too much has happened to be remembered. What would be the good to any one of your breaking your heart here and me mine in India? If any one is to expiate for wrong done, it's me and not you—it has nothing to do with you.'

'She was my friend. I always meant more to her than she to me. How I wish it had been the other way.'

'I am strong enough to carry your cares and my own.'

'But is it right,' she asked sobbingly, 'that our happiness should spring from her misery? I keep thinking, Stephen—I can't help it—I keep thinking what she would feel if she knew it were me. I keep hearing sentences she said once when she came here, the last time I saw her—they come out of nowhere and I can't get them out of my ears. I feel, even though she's dead, she's so unquiet.'

'Emmy,' he said authoritatively, 'that's superstitious, it's wrong to feel like that. The dead get right away, they've had their turmoil in this world, they don't remain here, clogged by this earth.'

'Perhaps,' she sobbed, her hands tightening on his, 'but what about the dead who have taken their own lives? Nannie would say they were tethered to this world until their foredoomed time comes to leave it.'

'You're not surely frightened by an old woman's tales?' he demanded. 'Look at it in this way: if she can see and feel us as you say, do you think it would bring her any happiness to know we were wretched and worn and apart?'

'Oh, Stephen,' she said, hiding her face, 'I think she would rather that than know we were together.'

'It's unjust to her to speak like that,' he said in agitation, 'wickedly unjust. After all, Emmy, happiness is good, not evil. God never said we were to be sad and unhappy; what does that achieve, anyway, but its own bitter frustrated ends? Isn't it better that happiness should come out of unhappiness instead of more pain? Listen, darling, we shall have to say and plan everything to-night for it would be wiser not to write to each other. I go home to-morrow to spend my last days with my mother. She suspects it was because of you I broke off my engagement; I don't know why when she only saw you once. We'll need to be married on Tuesday, Emmy, and it will need to take place at Fortgall because of Mr Cameron, my minister. I only wish I could come to Dormay for you, but that is impossible because of my mother and the time. Could you be in Dormay by eleven o'clock on Tuesday to catch the coach that leaves then for Fortgall? Lisbet, how can she reach Dormay?'

'The coach passes down this side of the loch on Tuesdays and Fridays,' I said, 'she could catch it when it passes the march gate about nine in the morning.'

'That would do, wouldn't it, Emmy? You'll arrive too soon in Dormay, but it's better to have too much time than too little. I will be in the square at Fortgall to meet you. We sail from the Clyde at dawn on Wednesday. Once we're married, we'll travel to Glasgow—we'll need every minute of our time. And you'll need money. Lisbet, this should be enough to take her to Fortgall.'

'Will we be married in a church, Stephen?'

'We can't be, Emmy, unless banns are cried, and that's impossible, but Mr Cameron, my minister, has consented to witness our marriage.'

'You mean he'll marry us?'

'Not actually marry us. We will simply require to take each other for husband and wife, by word of mouth, before witnesses. Any one, more or less, would do as a witness, but I knew it would make all the difference to you if Mr Cameron would agree to be one of them. They call it a half-mark or an irregular marriage—we aren't able to help that, Emmy—but it is legal and binding. Morally and legally, before God and man, we will be husband and wife. Nothing can part us once we are married.'

'No, nothing can part us once we are married,' she repeated.

He called her by name over and over again, his voice wild with longing. I stood, waiting for them, at the edge of the little beach where the burn grated the loose pebbles together and where I could feel the damp coming out of the stones of the bridge and chilling the air.

Every minute brought us nearer Tuesday, but Emmy and I spoke little about it, and when we did only when we were walking together outside. It was as though we were afraid if we did discuss it freely, our words would make her plans tangible enough to be discovered. Also the thought of the coming separation bound both our tongues; I could not think of it without a lump rising in my throat and my heart aching with misery. Emmy was ever sparing with her caresses, but during those few days I often found her hand holding mine.

Although the hours we were to be together shortened with every jerk of the clock's hand, the days dragged for both of us. The mental tumult Emmy was passing through exhausted not only her brain but her body; we were both keyed to so high a measure that our emotions played each moment into a minute and the days flagged by. I know I found myself mutely praying for Tuesday that, since it was coming to pass, it would come quickly.

On the Monday morning I was whipping up some whites of eggs for Nannie in the kitchen when Emmy called me upstairs.

'Beat up your whites here,' she invited me.

I stood with my back towards her to the window while I whipped the whites into snowy castles which hung to the plate when I turned it upside down.

'You have a very nice back,' she remarked after a few minutes.

'Have I?' I said, and laughed round at her.

'Yes,' she answered. 'You know, I suppose, it was as much my fault as his that I never liked Nicholas Strathern.

I daresay he's a great deal nicer than I have given him credit for.'

'What made you think of him just now?' I asked quickly.

'Oh, I don't know, nothing at all,' she replied, looking at her spread-out hand.

That afternoon we went for our last walk together. It was Nannie's washing-day and the wet clothes she had hung outside capered in the wind, making a whipping sound. We went on the moor which for me was haunted with memories of Julia and the dominie. Rain was passing in the distance and the sun, draining through heavy clouds, caught in an unreal radiance the grey rocks round us. It was April, but the screes and scaurs of the hills were still wridy, and we came upon a beautiful lost snow wreath lying in a hidden hollow of the moor. Emmy burst into a sudden storm of tears when she saw it.

'It makes me think of her,' she said, 'she was little and white.'

I had wanted to go with her on the morrow as far as Dormay. Fortgall was out of the question because there were no coaches back that day, but we both received an invitation from the Malcolms, asking us to join an excursion on Tuesday to visit the ruined Castle of Speyie. Emmy made me promise to go, for she knew if it were thought she was with me on the other side of the loch, her absence would be accounted for and her real whereabouts unsuspected.

Grely the morning dawned that she was to leave. I lay with eyelids still half-shut with sleep, watching the wardrobe form through the darkness, the mirror reflect wanly across the lightening room, and the dressing-table take shape at the window. What had looked like the humped form of a witch, I now saw was my clothes lying in a heap on a chair, for I had climbed into bed the previous night without folding them neatly as usual and without finishing plaiting my hair. Emmy's shoes stood in the fender; they looked lonely as all shoes somehow look lonely when they are empty of their trusting feet. Outside a faint misty rain was falling on the already humid earth.

I was to leave at half-past eight in the morning to be ferried over the loch by Duguid Wands, as the excursion was starting from Dr Malcolm's house at ten. We arranged between our two selves that Emmy would not leave the house with me, for we knew Mr Boyd set out for his morning walk immediately after breakfast and we were afraid of his seeing her. We settled for her to slip out at a quarter to nine, by which time he would be well on his way to Auchendee, the direction from which the coach was coming, and mamma would be helping Nannie to make papa's bed.

We went in to see papa immediately after breakfast; he feared we were not going to have a very good day for our outing, but told us to mark especially the cup-holed stone and the old pipers' gallery which we would see at the Castle.

I went back to our bedroom with Emmy, where I stood, knowing I should be gone yet not able to go. I could not raise my eyes from the gloves I kept pulling on to my fingers and when my voice did come it was barely a whisper.

'Emmy, darling, good-bye and God bless you.'

'Lisbet—you know I love you—Lisbet—'

I ran from the room. She did not go to the window to wave to me and I could not look back.

Duguid Wands helped me out of the rocking boat and I bade him good-night. A depression which foreshadowed something dire happening had weighed on me all day. It was because of this premonition that the nearer I drew to the manse, the slower my footsteps became, not only because I dreaded entering the house bereft of Emmy or giving papa and mamma her letter which I knew she had hidden for them under my pillow.

As I walked up the garden path, I had the uneasy impression I was being watched and waited for, and when I entered the manse, I saw Mr Boyd standing in the hall. I was feeling ill and unhappy, and he was the last person I desired to see at that moment. I gave him an inaudible greeting and was about to pass upstairs when he asked me if I would speak with him for a few minutes in the parlour. I had hardly time to be surprised. Once facing him in the parlour I saw he was labouring under some emotional stress, for he had difficulty in finding his voice, and I jumped to the conclusion that he had received bad news.

I was never more aware of any one's physical features as I was of Mr Boyd's. Although I knew it to be unjust, I could not divorce him from his mouth like a frog's and his hands padded with fat. Even now, when my pity was transiently aroused, I saw them.

'You are alone, Miss Lisbet?' he asked at last.

'Yes, yes,' I reassured him. 'What is the matter, Mr Boyd? You are in trouble.'

He did not answer but walked over to the window and stared out very intently, as though that gave him an excuse for standing there. He cleared his throat before remarking, quite pleasantly:

'Miss Emily would be with you to-day, of course.'

It was more the amiability of his tone than his actual words that bade me beware.

'No,' I answered steadily, 'she was not.'

'Indeed,' he replied, and I knew his surprise to be feigned, 'but I was under the impression, as was every one else in the house, that she was accompanying you.'

I could only say, 'Nevertheless she did not.'

'It is all in a piece with her deceit and double dealing,' he exclaimed, wheeling round on me, 'and you are every whit as bad as she—condoning and aiding as you have done.'

'I cannot see,' I told him, reinforcing myself with cold-ness, 'why my sister Emmy's movements should trouble you.'

'Do you believe,' he demanded, 'that any one will think well of a shameless girl, and because she is your sister acquits you of nothing, who is willing to go through a form of marriage with a man within three weeks of the death of—'

'Mr Boyd,' I interrupted fiercely, 'what my sister has done concerns you in no way. You are not asked to absolve her of blame or carry her conscience for her.'

'It has everything to do with me,' he answered. 'Whilst your father is indisposed, I am here in his place.'

I knew I was quibbling but I could not help myself. 'In what capacity?'

'To see that what would not happen if he were well enough to be up and about does not happen when illness has laid him aside.'

I did not realise then the full import of his words.

'There is a question that does concern us both, Mr Boyd,' I said, 'and that is how you have come by your information.'

'I am grateful—and you one day will thank me also, as your father would to-day if he knew—that I "came by" that information. It was meant that I should learn it.'

'And for what must we thank you?' I asked.

'That I was able to do what your father would have done in the circumstances: forbid your sister to go and take precautions that she did not leave the house.'

My feelings reached a pitch at that moment they never in a lifetime reached again. I knew then what it was to feel murder in one's heart. And I was only able to look at him, words I could not articulate battling to my throat.

'By so doing I prevented a trespass against our church, and saved your parents suffering from their daughter's misdemeanour, and, as your sister may one day come to realise, have saved her from herself, probably her own worst enemy. I did only what your father would have done.'

'Papa do what you have done!' My voice had risen hysterically and I had no power to lower it. 'Papa, the most honourable man on earth—eavesdrop as you must have done that evening—'

'Young misses should not make dishonourable plans and then they will not be discovered.'

My heart was missing beats, and I felt as though I were falling down interminable flights of invisible stairs. I groped in my mind for the purpose why he had done this thing, as though that alone would save my reason.

'Why did you do it?' I asked in a voice I could scarcely make audible and it was not really him I was asking, for I knew he would never give me the answer, knew that perhaps he himself did not know it. 'You must have had some reason—some justification—'

'The performing of my duty, however distasteful, is quite sufficient reason,' I heard him say; 'as for justification, my action calls for none. Of the three of you,' he was now speaking emphatically, as though repeating something he had learnt by heart, 'your sister Emily was the one I always liked the least and never approved of.'

His white collar gleamed through the gathering twilight. I was staring into his full pale eye as though I would find the answer to my question there; the man himself seemed to have fallen away from me for I saw only his eye.

'Here is the key of your bedroom.'

I think I struck out at him. I know I snatched the key from his hand, and, turning, ran from the room upstairs. The key, being rusty, took long to fit and turn in the lock, but at last I was standing in the darkened room where the shadows on the walls of the leafless branches outside were like lobsters fighting.

A strong draught came from the window and the door slammed loudly behind me. I called Emmy by name but the room was empty.

Our bedroom window had always been difficult to open, and when we wanted to air the room we raised the skylight. The window was now so jammed and sealed with disuse it could not be moved, but Emmy had managed to lever it up with her shoe-horn, breaking and splitting the wood round the frame, and, stuffing the bolster between it and the sill to keep it open, had escaped with the help of the fir tree outside. The drop from its lowest branch to the ground was considerable, but I knew she would hardly notice it.

I stood in the cold room, my heart beating unevenly. It was now four o'clock and I had left her after half-past eight. Mr Boyd had probably watched me leave the manse and, when I was well away, gone upstairs to our bedroom. I knew that in those circumstances it would be well-nigh impossible for Emmy to have caught the only coach that day from Mhoreneck to Dormay when it passed the march gate at nine.

Dormay was seven miles away and it was only there, at the inn from where the coaches left, that I could discover if she had been in time to board the Fortgall coach. I knew from the skirl in the wind and the way the trees shook in agitation that a storm was mounting. I shut the window and before I left the room something made me take Emmy's old thick cape with me.

It was dark when I reached Dormay; the shadows did not steal behind me but strode like marching men. Rain, which had been spitting on and off all afternoon, began to fall heavily. I felt it sting my face and chill my hands as I crossed the bridge over and river.

There were no lights in any of the inn's front windows

and I had to knock more than once before my summons was answered. At last I heard reluctant footsteps and the door was opened by a woman who stood looking down at me with the aggressive expression of one who resents interruption. In one hand she held a candle which she shielded from the wind with the other. Its smoky flame lit up her roughened face with its beaten-in brow and gaunt cheeks.

'Can you tell me,' I asked, 'if a girl in a brown cape and a velvet bonnet boarded the coach to-day which leaves for Fortgall at eleven?'

'That I can no,' she answered, and made to shut the door, but I darted forward and stood in the aperture.

'I must know,' I said, shouting at her above the wind, 'it is absolutely imperative I know. Perhaps your husband—or the man who looks after the horses— could tell me.'

'Ye had better come ben,' she replied, 'or ma candle will blaw oot.' Once the door was shut and we were standing in the draughty lobby, she peered curiously at me, her shadow towering unsteadily above her. 'A lass did come here this aifternoon,' she said, 'but I couldna tell ye whit she was for wearing.'

'Did she catch the coach?'

'Na, she didna. She babbled on aboot the coach that went to Fortgall until we were tired screaming at her it had left twa oor syne. Then she ca'ed for a carriage and horses, as if we had them harnessed and waiting for her in the yard, and when we told her we hadna them, she took the telling ill. Ma husband told her there was na way to get to Fortgall frae here the day, and she cried oot then aboot Glasgow. He told her the nearest she could get to Glasgow was Stirling, and he thocht a carriage passed through Kildour on its way to Stirling at three this aifternoon, but he wasna sure. Onywey she was o'er late for it. She asked him then was there na one in the whole o' Dormay wha would drive her to Kildour, and he said na one had the horses. Then she asked him which road went to Kildour, and when he told her, she turned, withoot a look or word to ony o' us, and

jigged doon the road. She would be sair-footed lang afore
she neared Kildour.'

'Which is the road she took?' I asked, and when I found
my voice had sunk to a whisper, I repeated it too loudly.

'The one to the west through the glen, but it's like a daft
body to gang alang it the nicht—ye'll no see onything
through this blatter o' storm.'

I ran from her down the road with the wind buffeting me
before it. I thought I saw, through the unreal dark, some one
coming towards me over a field, waving menacing arms, and
I shrieked in terror. The wind caught my cry and tore with it
to the ends of the world. My heart was still knocking within
me when I discovered the thing was merely a scarecrow.
Fear had only one wooden leg, and its empty arms flapped
helplessly in the wind; I overcame terror and rode on it
that night in the mile to the lighted toll-house.

A woman came to the door when I knocked, and told
me that some one, answering to my sister's description,
had been seen hurrying past that afternoon; she seemed
to know well enough where she was going. I asked if
she could possibly have reached Kildour by three and
the woman stared at me, then called over her shoulder
to some one within. We heard a chair scraping on the
floor and a bearded man, in his shirt sleeves, appeared
from the duskily glowing kitchen. They were kind but
slow of understanding, and my anxiety did not serve to
hasten them. When at last they understood my question,
the man shook his head and said:

'A coach couldna mak' Kildour in yon time, far less a lass.'

He put on his coat to come with me and brought his dog
and a lantern. I do not know how far we walked, but at the
march gate separating Taggart's land from MacDiarmid's
the toll-man stopped to say he would go on by himself
and that he should not have brought me so far, but I
was panic-stricken about Emmy and would not return by
myself to the toll-house. After that hummocks seemed to
grow into hills, and hills rose into mountains before me,
while the twisted roots of heather laid traps for my unwary

steps. There was sleet in the rain and the winds whipped it, hissing, through the glen. They made an angry tearing sound behind us, as if struggling in an invisible sheet. In the swaying light of the lantern the drops of rain looked ghostily enlarged.

My frantic prayers willing Emmy by some miracle to reach Stephen in time, my wild bargainings with God if only He would grant what I asked, had resolved themselves as the miles passed into the one monotonous phrase which repeated itself so often that it had now lost all meaning for me, 'Oh, God, keep her safe—oh, God, keep her safe.'

The dog whined. But for it we might have passed her unnoticed, for she was lying on the leeward side of a dyke. I ran up to her, stumbling in my haste, but I could hardly bring myself to look at her for fear of what I would see as I parted her hair which, out of curl, had blown across her face.

'Emmy,' I said, 'Emmy.'

In the lantern's light I saw her moist lids flutter. A spasm crossed her face and held it fixed; I think she aged in that moment as years could never have aged her, she who was still so like a wild rose carved out of stone. I put my arms round her to raise her from the sodden ground and felt the beads of rain which clung to her hair against my cheek like tears.

Our wet clothes slapped the floor when we took them off in the toll-house. We put Emmy to bed and the woman fed her with hot gruel to try to work some heat through her. She lay so still for Emmy that I was frightened and watched for the smallest movement to comfort me, but I only caught the glitter of her eyes through half-closed lids. Life beat within her like a moth fluttering in a hollow shell.

I was not in a state to cope with anything, and worked myself into a helpless fever thinking of the anxiety those at home would be enduring. I knew Mr Boyd would in all probability inform them of what had taken place, but he could not tell where either of us was. The toll-man said he would send one of his sons to the manse that night to let them know we were storm-stayed. I wanted to write a letter for him to take in which I would explain as well as I could what had happened, but there was no paper or writing materials in the cottage. The boy had to leave with a verbal message that we were both safe, but had got caught in the storm and could not return until the morrow. I did not dare think what they would feel when they learnt where we were.

I climbed into the bed beside Emmy; there were no sheets, but the blankets seemed bereft of all heat. And now she could not lie still but started at my side and sat up in bed, holding her head and muttering below her breath.

'I know what he's feeling—I feel what he's feeling—oh, if I were only dead and need never feel again. Yet I will remember even when I'm dead. This time yesterday I didn't know what was going to happen—if you could only get back, get back to that night under the bridge when he was beside me. Every minute is taking him farther and farther from me, and it might have been so different, it might have been so different. That man—I tell you, he's mad. Why did I never see he was hideous before? What went wrong, Lisbet, what went wrong? Was there too much against it, was that it? I'll never get my breath again. It's eleven miles to Kildour—only eleven short miles, and it's taken me so long to pass that tree.' Her voice cracked.

All night long the wind hung round the shuddering cottage which creaked and groaned like an old woman in a chair. Once a child cried out in its dreams and through the thin partition between us and the kitchen we could hear the frightening, unlikely nose noises of some one sleeping heavily.

I was up several times during the night, bringing Emmy water to drink. Before dawn I was awakened by her shivering so violently she shook the whole bed; it was as though she had an ague, for she could not stop trembling. I was terrified and lit the candle and brought her more water, the last I could find. The candle was but rudely made and burnt, crackling and flaring, like a small fire.

'Lisbet, do something to make me stop thinking—anything, anything, but do something; they're going so fast and I've got to keep up with them. They'll wear out my brain and keep on and on and round and round in nothing. I'm still running, Lisbet, that's what's wrong, and now he's gone—I know he's gone now, and he can hardly lift his head, and I have never run so fast and yet I'm standing still.'

There was a Bible lying on the window-sill. I picked it up and it fell open at the Psalms where it was evidently accustomed to being opened, for the tops of their thumbed pages were worn where the book-marker had passed often backwards and forwards. 'The sacrifices of God,' I read, 'are a broken spirit: a broken and a contrite heart, O God, Thou wilt not despise.' What did it mean, that terrible sentence, what did it mean? 'Some trust in chariots, and some in horses: but we will remember the name of the Lord our God.'

I read her out the twenty-third Psalm and, as her shaking was subsiding, I prayed she would fall asleep, but although her eyes remained closed, I knew she was still awake.

The toll-man's son returned early in the morning, for they kept him the night at the manse, and brought with him a letter from papa. It was addressed to us both, but I did not show it to Emmy; I do not think she would have comprehended it or cared if she had. He wrote that he had learnt from Mr Boyd what had happened, and he would make no comment at present. He gathered from the boy that Emily had caught a chill and he instructed us to stay where we were until Dr Malcolm called for us some time that day in his wagonette.

While we waited for the doctor, Emmy lay on top of the bed in the kitchen where it was warm and I sat on the settle. I noticed she was holding her thumbs and rose to put her hands under the sheets. The dog settled itself at my feet, with its narrow head lying on its paws and its unblinking eyes lit like rubies by the fire. That thatch covered many heads, for there were quite half a dozen small, shy, smiling children, who could speak no English, in the kitchen that morning. They all seemed alike to me, with the same round eyes and curious reddish-fair hair which looked as though it were freckled. They played quietly enough by themselves in a corner of the kitchen, from where I heard husky whispers, quickly stifled with laughter.

Dr Malcolm arrived for us about noon. He was a burly man who did not realise his own strength and who did everything, whether it were entering a room or saying good-morning or merely putting down his cup, with the vigour of a hearty giant. Perhaps because of this I had always thought of him as slightly preposterous. Now I found him so kindly and unquestioning, like a pillar of strength, that I felt I never wanted to let him out of my sight; I remember him still in my prayers.

He wrapped Emmy well up with rugs and scarves and brought us home. It seemed so long ago since yesterday when I had left the manse that I might have been returning to it now in another lifetime. I heard the leisured tick of the hall clock. In the parlour everything—the familiar window, the table set for a meal, the half-knitted shawl mamma was making for Julia's baby—was in its place. All was comfortable, orderly and quite sane.

It was at the beginning of May, when the thunder of the burn in spate filled the glen and we received Stephen Wingate's first heart-broken letter on his way to India, that Emmy died.

The north wind drove the sheep with their inquisitive, confiding lambs to the sheltered sides of dykes. Against the darkening sky the spring trees looked unreally bright. Snow scattered itself beside wondering primroses and pale withdrawn wind-flowers. The startled, reiterated cry of a cuckoo sounded as the flakes began to fall more thickly, blurring from view all but the nearest trees.

Aimless misshapen snowflakes floated against the window-pane we had seen sprinkled with spring rain in the morning. I watched them silently cake the sill as I sat beside Emmy, while we heard from downstairs the occasional murmur of voices, or the opening and shutting of a door.

Earlier in the day I think she had felt everything was closing in upon her, cornering her in bed, caging her for all perpetuity to a tired body. But now it was as though she had detached herself from the world with its futile winds. Consequences and fulfilment no longer disturbed her. The voices from downstairs were merely little puffs that rose only to be drowned in an immense silence, the seasons were but vagaries passing fitfully by, and the life of the moth she saw clinging to the floor, its colourless wings spinning, was as extended as her own.

We sat up with her that night, for she was tied to life only by a tugging breath. At the end we went forward to raise her in our arms, but she motioned us away with her hand. I think she thought there was something unseemly in this struggle for breath. Even after she was dead, her face quivered and the pulse in her neck leapt, as a feather sometimes gives semblance of life.

# Epilogue

Hay waved again waist high at the march gate and pansies bordered the beds in the Gows' wintry garden—she always thought pansies had such cross wee faces. Bluebells grew in the little mossy places she knew so well and the yellow tormentil starred the turf on the old drove road over the hills.

Julia and Edwin never returned to the house out of Dormay, overlooking the river, and we left the manse between Barnfingal and Auchendee that August, for the Highland climate was thought too rigorous now for papa. We decided to move to Glasgow to be near Julia, and papa received a call to Mr Miller's church beside the Green which had been a Relief Church before the Union in 1847.

The evening before we left Barnfingal I went by myself for a walk. A scattering of birds flew out as lightly as blown leaves when I went up the path, butterflies' wings blinked in the shadows and a dragon-fly pursued me, its head like an eye. I walked on the moors where the winds roam eternally free. When I returned the shadow of each newly-made haystack in Gow's field stretched to its neighbour, as if their spirits were trying to reach out one to another. From the edge of the field marguerites stared, their petals drawn back from their yellow faces, as though scared at something they had seen pass.

Next day we left the manse with curtainless windows and uncarpeted stairs, squares of dust where heavy furniture had stood and unfaded spaces on the walls where pictures had once hung. I felt in some dim way we were abandoning it; but as I looked back for the last time, I had the impression that the empty house devoid of life had never been more full before, that unseen eyes gazed from the vacant windows, and the landing still creaked although no footsteps passed over it.

We climbed into the carriage waiting for us at the gate. Mamma's face was bedimmed with tears but papa was pre-occupied opening a parcel of books on his knees to reassure himself that he had not forgotten a certain volume.

'We will never manage,' he said pessimistically, strug-gling to tie the string, 'never in this world, with all these bundles and packages and basket of bottles and your moth-er's hat-box, if that young man isn't there as he said he would be.'

'Of course he will be there,' I assured him hurriedly, feel-ing responsible, for he referred to Nicholas Strathern who had promised to meet the carriage at Dormay and travel to Glasgow with us to help us on the journey. I could see him in my mind's eye standing, tall and reliable, with his watch in his hand, telling us exactly how many minutes we were late before he kissed me.

The carriage moved forward. We turned the bend in the road where we used to stand to see if any one were coming. I heard the immeasurable murmur of the loch, like a far-away wave that never breaks upon the shore, and the cry of a cur-lew. All the world's sorrow, all the world's pain, and none of its regret, lay throbbing in that cry.

We came upon Barnfingal and left it behind us with its cottages lying like quartz pebbles at the foot of the mountains. The last glimpse I had of it was of the raised, hummocked graveyard on the hill, with its grey gravestones all blankly facing east.

CANONGATE CLASSICS
TITLES IN PRINT